THE ORCHID

London, 1840: When Ava Miller's father died, she promised she would continue to run The Orchid Theatre and look after its close-knit family of actors. But when Henry Scott-Leigh, the son of the wealthy owner of the theatre, turns up one day threatening to replace Ava or close the unprofitable business altogether, the future looks bleak. Can Ava make a success of the next play and save everything she loves? And what will come of the growing attraction she and Henry share, when they inhabit such different worlds?

LUCY OLIVER

◆

THE ORCHID

Complete and Unabridged

LINFORD
Leicester

First published in Great Britain in 2015

First Linford Edition
published 2015

A catalogue record for this book is available
from the British Library.

ISBN 978–1–4448–2625–8

Published by
F. A. Thorpe (Publishing)
Anstey, Leicestershire

Set by Words & Graphics Ltd.
Anstey, Leicestershire
Printed and bound in Great Britain by
T. J. International Ltd., Padstow, Cornwall

This book is printed on acid-free paper

1

The Orchid Theatre, London, 1840

A loud rap echoed from the door and Ava sighed. She'd have preferred to remain undisturbed while she checked the theatre account books, hoping against all hope that this time they would show a profit. So far, she'd had no joy. It was clearly stated in black ink that since she'd taken over managing the theatre, their takings had halved.

The knock sounded again. Ava put down her pen. 'Yes?'

The door opened and her assistant manager, Clarence, looked in. His blond hair was ruffled as if he had been anxiously pulling it, and a heavy overcoat hid his small frame.

'There's a man to see you,' he said. 'Posh chap.'

'Patron or playwright?'

'Neither.'

'Then tell him to return at a more convenient time. I expect it is a salesman.' She looked back down at her books.

Clarence coughed. 'Ava, he says he owns the theatre.'

'What?' Her brow creased. 'Is it Mr Scott-Leigh? He hardly ever comes here.'

'It's not the old chap, but I reckon it could be one of his sons.'

Ava stood up. It would be easier if Clarence asked people's names when they arrived, but he considered opening the door to be beneath him. Though to be fair, she had made it clear to her acting staff that they were not domestic servants. Which Scott-Leigh was it though? There were three brothers, but since the middle one was in the army it must be either Jasper or Charles. She tightened her lips, not relishing the thought of dealing with either of them. If only she owned the theatre outright, then she would be answerable to no one.

Smoothing down her dark-print working gown, she took a small hat from the stand by the door and followed Clarence. In the corridor, she shivered at the vicious November wind blowing through the gaps in the ill-fitting doors and windows. In this damp building she needed a fire in every room, but until they got a sell-out show, there was no way she could afford it.

'I've put him in there.' Clarence pointed to the parlour room, which Ava used for auditions and meeting writers. Smiling, she touched his arm as she went past. Dear Clarence, she couldn't have run this theatre without him. Even though she couldn't afford to pay him, he stayed on in return for bed and board. It was impossible to imagine The Orchid without him; her father had employed him as an errand boy many years ago.

'Have you asked Cook to bring the tea?' she said.

He shook his head. 'Is Mr Scott-Leigh intending on staying for long?'

'I wouldn't know, since I've not yet spoken to him. But we must be polite as he's travelled far to see us, and while I doubt he has good news, we will do our duty as hosts.'

'Be careful, Ava. I don't trust this man.'

'You never trust anyone.' She patted his arm fondly. 'You think they're all out to harm me.'

'I saw the state you were in after William ran off, and I don't want to see you hurt again.'

'Well, Mr Scott-Leigh is here purely on business. He's not going to break my heart.' Ava smiled.

Pushing open the door to the parlour, she strode in. Her guest stood with his back to her as he warmed his hands at the tiny fire. His long coat, stretched across wide shoulders, dripped water onto the rug and his boots were stained with mud. It appeared he had travelled by horseback, unusual in this weather for a man of his station.

She coughed. 'Sir?'

The figure turned around and she jerked back, raising a hand to her mouth to stifle her gasp. It wasn't Jasper or Charles. This man — with a long, dark red scar that raised the corner of his mouth towards his cheek — was a stranger.

'You needn't try and hide your shock. I know what I look like,' he said. 'It is fitting that I am in a theatre, is it not, when I look like the main character from a grisly murder play.'

'You do not, sir,' she said truthfully. He was badly scarred, that she couldn't deny, but above the twisted injury his eyes were intelligent and the colour of a conker shell in autumn. The hollowed cheeks and pale skin, however, testified to a long illness.

'I am Miss Miller,' she said.

He bowed. 'Henry Scott-Leigh.'

Ava sat down on the sofa, wiggling as the broken springs pushed up against her bottom. Henry was the middle brother. Someone knocked on the door and she leant over to pull open the handle.

'Tea?' Daisy said, bobbing a curtsey.

Ava wished she wouldn't. Everyone at The Orchid helped out with other jobs, but that didn't mean Daisy had to act like a cowed servant.

'Thank you,' Ava said, standing up to take the tray and placing it on the table. Glancing at it, she nodded. Cook had at least used the decent tea pot, even if the sandwiches looked dry and under-filled. Setting out two cups, she poured as Henry strode to look from the window.

'Milk or lemon?' she said.

'What? Oh, lemon please, and sugar.'

Thankfully, he sat down in the chair opposite, as all his pacing about was irritating. Whatever he was here for, he didn't look comfortable. It was clear he was about to impart bad news and she had a very good idea of what that news might be. Her hands trembled as she handed him a cup. Please don't let him close The Orchid. It was the only home she had ever known. And what would happen to the motley crew of actors who had become her family? Nausea rose from her stomach and she swallowed.

Henry cleared his throat. 'I'm here to sort out the running of the theatre. Since your father sadly passed away, our profits have dipped alarmingly.'

Ava moistened her lips, not daring to move in case she fainted. 'I'm sorry for the reduced payments, but I can assure you the drop in income is only temporary. We've got some good shows planned.'

'It's got nothing to do with your shows. You have lost many of your patrons because their wives do not feel that The Orchid is the respectable establishment it once was.'

'I don't have prostitutes drifting about my premises.' She wasn't even gratified to see his cheeks flush at her use of the word. Really! Did he think she was a complete innocent?

He coughed. 'People aren't happy about the theatre being run by a woman, and a single woman at that.'

'But I have always helped my father with The Orchid, and I ran it successfully during his final illness.'

'It's not considered appropriate for you to manage such a business alone.'

'Is this the opinion of the patrons, or your own?'

His jaw tightened. 'It is the opinion of everyone I have spoken to. You shouldn't have just taken over when your father died. My family own the theatre and it is our place to put in a manager.'

She gripped the settle, fingers whitening. 'You are ordering me out because I am a woman?'

'My family invest in theatres, music halls and breweries; we pride ourselves as a family business and guard our reputation well. We can't be associated with a theatre that is both failing and of ill repute.'

'Ill repute?' She jumped up.

8

'Please, sit down. I appreciate the situation is not of your doing, but that is the word on the street.' He eyed her. 'And a good theatre manager ought to have been aware of it.'

'I haven't heard these slanderous rumours because I don't frequent taverns or coffee houses,' Ava said, teeth clenched. 'I spend my evenings sewing and reading. Yet a man can drink, keep mistresses and still be considered a suitable person to employ.'

'That is the way of the world, I am afraid.'

'So what is to happen to me? The workhouse?'

'My sister is in need of a lady's maid. You're used to helping actresses dress and do their hair, are you not?'

Ava looked at him, trembling in anger. 'Not just actresses, I dress actors too — handing them their breeches and straightening their collars.'

He jerked back and she closed her eyes. Why had she said that? It would only prove to him that she was the immoral woman he believed her to be. It was too late to take it back though. But hopefully it would make him realise that she wouldn't be a suitable servant to his sister.

'Then perhaps I should employ you as my valet, since you are so well versed in the dressing habits of men.' The corner of his lip turned up slightly.

Ava raised her chin with dignity. 'I do not believe that would be considered suitable, sir.'

'I will therefore search for alternative employment for you.'

'As a governess, or seamstress?'

'No one would employ an ex-actress to teach their children. Can you sew?'

Her lips tightened; he was playing with her. 'Go and check the costume wardrobe, since we make the outfits ourselves here. But I can assure you, Mr. Scott-Leigh, that I won't accept any employment you have found me. This theatre is my home, and the people here my friends. I have no others. If you throw me out I will sit on

10

the doorstep in my rags, cursing your name and scaring away the patrons.'

'Then you will find yourself in a prison cell.'

'And your conscience could live with that? You would drag a woman from her home and throw her into prison?'

'If The Orchid doesn't make money soon, you'll be in Marshalsea prison anyway. Do you not understand how precarious your position is? I have looked into it. You have debts in your own name, and creditors threatening to take you to court. How well can you run a theatre from a debtors' gaol?'

Ava froze. Henry spoke the truth — her debts kept her awake at night, the figures dancing in her brain as she fell into fitful sleep, before waking to the imagined clash of the prison's iron gates. It would be easiest to let Henry take over the theatre. But she'd promised her father she'd look after The Orchid and its people, to run it as he did with a firm but kind hand. She couldn't give up now. Profits would improve when people realised she wasn't a wanton woman. Maybe she ought to marry? Some handy chap who'd leave her to run the place, whilst living at his club.

'What if I were married?' she said. 'Could I stay to run the theatre then?'

He eyed her. 'Are you engaged?'

Raising her head, she looked straight at him. 'A man has asked me to marry him, yes.' It wasn't a complete lie. She didn't need to mention that William had run off shortly afterwards.

'And have you agreed to wed this man?'

'I did.'

He inhaled sharply, then cleared his throat. 'Who is the gentleman and when is the big day?'

Ava gasped.

'Have you forgotten his name?'

'No, it's . . . Clarence.' She could explain to Clarence later that she had to do it to keep The Orchid. Hopefully he wouldn't mind too much; he was a single man.

'I had no idea of this relationship. Clarence lives on the premises, does he not?'

Ava swallowed. She'd forgotten that. Now it looked like she had no morals at all.

'Clarence stays in the men's quarters at the other side of the theatre and I share my floor with the girls. It is all above-board.'

'If it is all so above-board, why have you kept it hidden? I have seen no advertisement of your engagement.'

'Why would I advertise? I am not of your class. I do not habitually put personal messages in *The Times*. I'm not hiding anything.' Ava moistened her lips, cheeks warming. Lying never came easy to her, but she had to save the theatre. 'It changes things if I am to wed though, doesn't it? Clarence and I can run The Orchid together.'

'So you are intending to promote him to your position?'

'Of course not.'

'And you are confident that your

13

marriage wouldn't suffer by having your husband work for you?'

'But it would be all right for me to work for him?'

'It is more usual.'

'Well, I am not going to give up the management of The Orchid. And Clarence would not expect me to.'

Henry's lips turned upwards. 'I can see that, madam. It appears you're willing to go to immense lengths to keep the place. I'm impressed by your devotion, but that doesn't change the fact that the theatre is making no money.'

Ava stared at him. Was he going to close them down? He mustn't! She couldn't imagine herself living any-where else. And what would happen to her actors — the friends she had grown up alongside?

'Please, give me longer. I'm in the process of acquiring a new comedy script, which I know will make money. I know the theatre and how to run one. We've just been unlucky. But once we

14

find a good play, people will return.'

He gazed at her thoughtfully. 'And how do you intend to pay for this new script?'

'I have a bracelet my father left me.'

'You'd pawn your father's gift?'

Ava jerked her head up. How dare he suggest she was neglecting her father's memory. It was due to her memories that she was so desperate to keep the theatre running.

'He left me many gifts,' she said. 'Jewellery is not the most important one.'

Henry took a deep breath and looked around the room. 'All right, you can put on one more play, but I'm going to stay here to oversee it. You need to keep an eye on your costs, which are too high.'

'Clarence and I don't take a salary.'

'If a business can't provide enough income to give a living wage to those working in it, then it shouldn't survive. You and the assistant manager are to draw a wage, I insist upon that.'

'Insist?'

'Yes, insist. This theatre is under my control now and you will follow my orders. Until you can make a profit or are shut down, I'm going to stay here.'

Ava slumped down on the sofa, legs trembling. Surely he didn't intend to sleep here? Not after what he'd said about her lack of morals? She would never have a moment free from him.

'Stay?'

'Stay.'

'Is that decent?' she said. 'Wouldn't it be more appropriate for you to stay at your club?'

'I don't think your reputation will suffer for it. You're running a business, which by its very nature dances along the edge of morality. I doubt my presence will change much.'

She stood up. 'Get out! I am not lacking in morals. I am an honest and honourable woman.'

His mouth softened. 'I didn't mean to upset you. But your takings have suffered because people are concerned about a single woman working in the theatre, and you live in a mixed house with your actors. I apologise for talking out of turn, but I am thinking of you as well of the theatre. Your father served us faithfully for many years and the least I owe him is to take care of his daughter.'

'I don't need taking care of.' Her hands clenched into fists. Did she really have to work with this man? He'd veto her every suggestion. What did he know about working in the theatre? She looked at him. 'Since you are taking over The Orchid, I assume you have relevant experience?'

'Actually, I have never worked in this industry before.'

'Yet you believe you can do a better job than I? When I have been treading the boards for years?'

'I will leave the creative side to you so I can concentrate on the finances. I've been in the army for many years running my own garrison, so I know how to manage costs and people. I'm sure running The Orchid would not be so different.'

'My actors won't jump when you command and neither will I. Maybe you'd better return to the army.'

He winced and Ava bit her lip. What a cruel thing to say! He clearly hadn't left by choice. Not only did he have the damaged cheek, but when he paced about the room it was with a stiff back and right leg. Under his clothes, he was likely a mass of scars.

'I apologise,' she said. 'I spoke out of turn. I do understand that you are trying to help us.'

Henry looked away and when he spoke, his voice was muffled. 'I can't go back. A musket ball remains close to my spine. It was too dangerous to remove.'

Her eyes widened. 'Is it safe?'

'That depends on if it moves.' Touching his hat, he bowed. 'Goodbye, madam. I'll return after collecting my bags from my lodgings.'

Open-mouthed, she watched him stride from the room, then sank onto the sofa. This really wasn't what she wanted — to have her every decision questioned by a man who knew nothing of the theatre. And how dare he suggest that she lacked morals! The only men she associated with were those who worked for her.

Thinking of her actors, Ava remembered Clarence. She'd better let him know he was getting married — hopefully he wouldn't mind; he loved The Orchid as much as she did.

There was a soft knock at the door and her assistant manager looked in, his face pale. 'I heard arguing,' he said. 'Are you all right?'

'I'm fine, but I have news for you.' She relaxed, comforted by his familiar presence. No matter what changes were about to happen at The Orchid, Clarence would always remain the same. Her best friend and confidant.

'You and I are to be wed, Clarence!' she said, smiling.

He startled and Ava laughed.

'I had to tell Henry that we were going to marry, since it was the only way he would allow me to keep The Orchid. We will have to pretend to be engaged until he goes home.'

'I would be honoured to marry you.' He bowed.

Ava smiled and reached over to pat his hand. 'Dear Clarence, I honestly couldn't run this place without you.'

'So what is Mr Scott-Leigh intending to do?' he said.

'He's going to stay here to command us until we make a profit, which, from the current state of our booking list, could take some time. We need a hit show if we're ever going to be able to run ourselves again. In fact, if we can't increase our takings in a few months, we will all be out of a job. Mr Scott-Leigh has already offered me a position as lady's maid to his sister.'

'I can't see you as a lady's maid.' He grinned.

She sighed. 'Neither can I, but thankfully the position is no longer available since he believes me to be an immoral woman.'

Clarence's mouth tightened. 'A soldier and a gentleman dared to cast aspersions on your character, when I see most of his ilk in the brothels of an evening?'

She looked at him. 'What are you doing in brothels, Clarence?'

'Only walking past, my lady. I hate those places — full of dirty, diseased women. No, I prefer to spend my evenings at home, reading to you in the parlour.'

'I suppose the reading might have to stop now.' She frowned. 'I'm not sure Henry would approve of all of us mixing in the evening as we do at present. Maybe I should be a proper lady, sitting by myself with only Daisy for company.'

'Then Mr Scott-Leigh's visit will appear to last even longer than it does, as Daisy isn't known for her riveting conversation. You'll be discussing her new hat ribbons for hours.'

'Very true. Perhaps we'd better keep things as they are — in truth he can't think worse of me than he does at present. What does it matter if he believes me to have poor morals? As long as I am a married woman, all appearances will have been satisfied.'

'I wouldn't control you.'

'Clarence, we won't really be wed!' Standing up, she dusted her hands off; it really was time to clean the parlour again. 'I must prepare a room for our guest. I think the one at the top of the stairs is free.'

'Don't make him too comfortable, else you'll never get rid of him. I'd go for the one above the kitchen that gets the full force of Cook shouting at her range every morning and the clatter of hooves from the milk dray.'

'It's also quite dark and damp if I remember. I do believe you're right, Clarence. I think it would suit our unwanted visitor admirably.'

2

Henry yanked the drawer out and inspected the runners. They were broken, like everything else in this place. Dropping it into a corner of the room, he placed his cufflinks in a small lidded pot, which he closed and placed at an exact right angle on the bedside table. Finished with his unpacking, he cautiously lowered himself onto the bed. He had gone for a long ride this morning and his back ached. A pinging sound came from beneath him and he sighed as a spring stuck into his right buttock. The gas lamps were low, casting a circle of yellow light on the walls and bringing a welcome warmth as hailstones rattled against the ill-fitting window.

Was this a deliberate ploy to get him to leave? Certainly his father hadn't mentioned the place being so damned uncomfortable when he visited. Ava would have to try harder than this, though, if she wanted to drive him out; he'd spent the last six months living in a tent in the desert, the sun baking through the canvas. Though — he shifted as a dull pain spread over his shoulders — that had been before he was injured. Ava had looked shocked when she saw him, and whether that was due to her not expecting him, or from the scars on his face, he'd never know.

At least she hadn't looked disgusted like some people. Closing his eyes, he thought about the girl at the theatre last night who'd moved the folds of her dress away to stop them touching him. Women were best kept away from, and when he finally gave in to pressure from his father to find a bride, he'd select a quiet girl whom he could greet at breakfast and dinner. There'd be no risk of him getting hurt again.

Henry closed his eyes, remembering the pain of Harriet's betrayal. He had considered her a devoted fiancée, but whilst he recovered from his wounds, she'd been penning missives to Henry's own cousin. She'd been bored, she said, and anxious about Henry's health. The illicit love affair had been a distraction.

Sighing, he stretched; at least he had discovered Harriet's character before they'd wed. Although in the year since her betrayal, he had been unable to speak to another woman without wondering what secrets she kept. If he had been fooled by Harriet, a clergyman's daughter, what hope did he have of finding a faithful woman?

His thoughts drifted towards Ava and he shook his head, smiling. Not only was she engaged, but she was the complete opposite of what he wanted in a wife. Far too fiery and opinionated. Considering she had been brought up in a theatre, he'd expected a tart like the ones that hung around the doors of music halls. Granted, her morals must be lax since she openly shared her house with several men, but she'd been soberly dressed and polite in her speech. Very pretty too, with her auburn hair peeking out from under her hat and smooth, clear skin, which he had been tempted to touch. Likely he was drawn to her because his own flesh was so damaged, whilst she was whole and beautiful.

A year ago he wouldn't have even considered her morals, but Harriet had changed him. Now he looked at every woman with distrust, and Ava, with her casual living arrangements, was a clear target for his displeasure. It was unfair, he knew, because she had done nothing wrong. He would have to be careful not to paint every woman's character black due to Harriet's betrayal.

He swung his legs down, rubbing his spine. It was unlikely the household budget would run to medicinal baths here, so he'd have to use the public ones to soothe the pain. Now it was time to go downstairs and talk to Ava about her plans for the theatre. She didn't want him here, but then she wasn't aware of how lucky she had been to keep her job. Part of Henry's instructions from his father had been to replace her with an experienced male manager.

His failure to dismiss her meant they would now have to work together. Henry sighed; Ava would not be easy to manage. Perhaps he should tell her he had changed his mind? Then remembering her wide, tear-filled eyes, he shook his head. The Orchid meant too much to her and he had to give her a chance. It had been devastating when he'd been dismissed from the army after so many years, and he hadn't grown up there. It would be worse for Ava.

Striding out of the door, Henry headed downstairs, grabbing the hand-rail as the worn carpet slipped under his boots. The stairs weren't the only hazard. He glanced at the chunks of plaster missing from the walls. Why was The Orchid so run-down? The profits during her father's management had been good, yet the theatre didn't look like it had seen a workman for years.

Reaching a long corridor, he opened a narrow green baize door and shivered as an icy cold wind blasted down the hall. From the muted laughter and conversation, he must be heading in the right direction though. His boots clattering on the flagstone floor, Henry breathed in the smell of damp and mould and noticed two doors open in front of him. Voices came from the first one, and he looked around the frame.

Inside the room, three girls clad only in corsets and bloomers were seated on stools. Their pale-skinned necks glowed under their twisted-up hair, which had been studded with tiny diamonds that gleamed under the candlelight. Standing behind Daisy with a hairbrush, Ava wore a velvet bodice with tiny seed pearls lined up the front, beneath which her long, slim legs stretched covered in only white stockings with pale blue garters.

Henry gasped, and she turned her head.

'This is the ladies' dressing room. Out!'

'I do apologise. So sorry, ladies. I didn't realise.' He turned his back. 'The door was open.'

'Go to the men's room next door. Clarence is there; he can assist you.'

Henry went quickly down the corridor. What a mistake to make! He hadn't expected to be met with such a display less than a day into his new job. Why had the door been left open? What had been happening in this theatre? It wasn't uncommon for places like this to double up as brothels and houses of ill-repute. What if Ava wasn't the struggling manageress he assumed, but a madam?

His fists clenched. If that was the case, he'd shut the place down immediately. There was no way his family's name was being sullied by being involved in such a business, no matter how lucrative.

Lips pressed together, he strode into the men's room, where Clarence sat in a burnished suit with a short skirt, beside a man in a Roman general's outfit. Two boys sat on stools, clutching sheets of paper.

'What's on tonight?' Henry said.

'*Antony and Cleopatra*,' Clarence said shortly. 'Come on lads, time to get backstage. Got all your lines memorised?' He strode out without waiting for an answer. Both boys dropped their scripts to the floor and scrambled after him.

The Roman general smiled and held out his hand, the first kind gesture Henry had been shown since he arrived. He'd met friendlier enemy armies than the occupants of The Orchid.

'I'm Walter,' the man said, his brown eyes large and smiling, reminding Henry of a border collie dog. 'We're due on stage now, but follow me and I'll find you a place to watch from the wings.'

'Thank you. I'm Henry Scott-Leigh.'
He bowed.

'I believe you're here to save us from certain collapse? Or to close us down, depending on whom I talk to.'

Henry straightened. Which comment had been made by Ava?

Walter grinned. 'I'd been expecting a visit from those above — I can spot the gaps in an audience as well as Ava. We all know The Orchid is struggling.'

'How long have you worked here?'

'Thirty years. I arrived at the tender age of ten as a workhouse errand boy. We're all life's rejects here. But we're a family now and I couldn't imagine being anywhere else. To you this is a small, struggling theatre, but to us it is our home and the place of our dreams. Think of that before you close us down.'

Henry took a deep breath. 'I want to keep you open, but if the theatre isn't making any profit there's nothing I can do.'

'You'll do your best though?'

'Of course I will.'

Walter smiled and held out his hand to shake. 'Then you are welcome, sir. Now follow me, since the performance is about to start.'

Henry stepped after Walter up a short flight of stairs, leading to the wings of the stage. Walter touched his finger to his lips, then crept away. Blinking to adjust his vision to the shadows, Henry stood still. In front of him, a heavy crimson curtain hung to the ground with pinpricks of light shining through the fabric. A stench of gas from the flickering lights filled the air and he winced. It would have been a relief to open a window, even though the air was still cold enough to numb his fingers. First, then, he needed to organise heating, as people wouldn't pay to sit in a freezing theatre all night.

A thud echoed from the stage and the two boys from the dressing room appeared, dragging two flat painted boards, which they set up to divide the stage into two. Squinting into the darkness, Henry made out pictures of pyramids and green hissing snakes that had been painted enthusiastically, but with little talent. A proper stage team would need to be employed. Compared to the spectacular Drury Lane, The Orchid looked like a provincial theatre — but, situated as it was in the West End, it had to be professional.

Henry would do his best, as he'd promised, but he couldn't be expected to keep open a failing company. Could he save this place? He must! It was his only chance to prove to his father that he could be successful in business. His fingers touched his scar. With his injuries he could get no other job, and living the empty life of a gentleman would destroy him.

Exhaling, Henry stared at the empty set in front of him. Where would he start? He knew little about theatres. Yet he knew he had good business sense, and Ava could surely be relied on to direct the actors. She must be an experienced manager, but seemed to lack the ability to control her costs. They could work well together, but she and her staff would have to stop their resentment of him. They weren't the polished, obedient soldiers he was used to though, so he would have to act with care and move slowly.

The faint lights glowing in the auditorium dimmed and he turned back to face the stage, as Walter and Clarence stepped out.

'Nay,' Walter said, 'but this dotage of our general's o'erflows the measure.'

Henry narrowed his eyes as he watched the two men. It was obvious, even to him, that they could act. Ava and her father had trained them well. Smiling, he leant back against the wall to watch as his leg ached, envying the audience their seats.

A thud echoed beneath the stage and Henry glanced quickly. Hopefully the floorboards weren't about to give way as victims to the dry rot and damp that riddled The Orchid. No, a trap door had slid open in the centre of the stage and a familiar woman with rich auburn tresses emerged through the floor, her smooth shoulders glowing under the gas lamp. As he stared, Ava flicked her green gown straight with one swift movement of her hand and his mouth fell open.

'If it be love indeed, tell me how much,' she said.

Henry shivered, staring. It must be the make-up that transformed Ava from an attractive woman into the queen before him with head held high, painted eyes slanted and cheek bones shaded. Flushing, he remembered offering her the position of lady's maid. Ava wouldn't need work to be found for her; she could walk into Drury Lane and be offered a part. Yet she chose to stay in this run-down hovel, performing on stage to drunks. Did she stay out of loyalty to her father? What had happened to her mother? Had she died? All he knew was that they hadn't been married and that Ava, for all her beauty and grace, was illegitimate.

Leaning back against the wall, he watched her. Gold shoes flickered under her dress and dimmed lights shone from her glossed hair. Truly, she made a splendid Cleopatra. Then his gaze dropped to her low-cut dress and he looked away. Did she have to wear such a garment? Hopefully she wasn't selling herself from this dark, run-down stage. She was worth so much more.

A bang sounding like a pistol shot echoed from the stage and Henry jerked, heart pounding and sweat breaking out across his forehead. Then the audience laughed and he swallowed, closing his eyes. The noise had been to simulate a Roman battle scene. He wasn't back out on the battle field again, fighting for his life. Breathing deep, Henry leaned back against the wall. It was no wonder his family had been relieved to send him to London, when he reacted like this. They didn't understand that after seeing young men blown into pieces and rivers of blood creeping across the sand, it was hard to settle back into a normal life. Even though he understood the worries of the actors at The Orchid, it was hard to compare their fears with what he had seen in battle; he had become hardened.

The curtain swung back across the stage, followed by very brief applause, then Clarence and Walter stepped back into the wings, the assistant manager already removing his armour. Without the protective metal shell and in only his shirt sleeves, he seemed smaller and somehow insignificant. Henry glanced away. So this was the man Ava intended to wed? It was hard to imagine them together, her beauty and vitality beside a man who seemed only to scowl. Hopefully he would treat her kindly; Henry had seen too many quiet men act as tyrants behind their own front doors.

But what did he know of love? Harriet had been a poor choice. Ava had known Clarence for years and understood his character far better than Henry did.

Walter cleared his throat. 'Are you joining us for a drink during the interval, Mr Scott-Leigh?'

Clarence stiffened and Henry narrowed his eyes.

'Thank you, I would love to,' he said.

'We're joining the women in their dressing room.' Walter grinned. 'I believe you know where it is.'

'I hope that mistake won't be made again,' Clarence said.

'It was unintentional.' Henry remembered Ava in her stockings as he followed the other two men from the stage.

Gas lights had been lit in the small dressing room and the woman were wrapped in robes and perched on stools, while yellow flames from a small fire reflected in the long mirrors. Ava looked up at Henry, then a kettle hung over the flames bubbled and she turned to lift it off.

'Sit down,' Walter said, tapping Henry

on the shoulder and pointing to a stool. 'We all meet in here to save on the expense of two fires.'

Ava glanced over her shoulder, with her heavily shadowed eyes glowing in the dim light.

'We've got beer, Mr Scott-Leigh, if tea isn't your drink?' she said.

Henry rubbed his numb hands. 'Tea will be most welcome, thank you.'

He sat down beside Daisy, whose silk stockings showed beneath her loosely tied robe. It was strange how quickly the abnormal became acceptable. None of the other men appeared concerned at all; in fact they both appeared more interested in the fruit cake Ava was now slicing. For now Henry would accept the situation, but when he had arranged sufficient funds he'd ensure a second fire was lit in the men's dressing room.

'Tea,' Ava said, handing him a cup. 'Have you met everyone now?'

'We haven't been introduced,' the girl sitting next to Daisy said, eyeing him. 'I'm Katie.'

'I'm Henry Scott-Leigh,' he said. 'My family own the theatre and I'm here to oversee the business.'

'Are you going to shut us down?' Daisy said.

Henry looked at her. Daisy was younger than he had thought, with her face still bearing the pink circles of adolescent spots. But her eyes were thickly lashed and expressive, showing the promise of beauty. She turned her head away from him, skin reddening. Likely, he had embarrassed her by walking into the dressing room by mistake earlier, although it was only Ava's figure that he remembered.

'I don't want to shut you down,' he said. 'But you must all be aware that The Orchid is verging on bankruptcy.'

'We're doing our best,' Katie said.

A few years older than Daisy, Katie smelt of perfume and hot sweat and Henry drew in a sharp breath. The girl reminded him of Harriet — all sensual promise. But life would be hard for Katie, since in her wide, laughing eyes there were no shadows of a pain that might have taught her caution.

A cough came from the corner of the room and Henry frowned. Huddled on a chair beside the fire sat a thin, silent figure.

'Amelia,' Ava said, nodding.

Henry stared at the girl. If Amelia washed her face and combed her hair, she could have been considered attractive. But huddled in a tartan wrap, with sharp cheekbones hollowing her face, she looked like an etching of a starving child from a charity poster. Then his lips tightened. Amelia's hands were trembling in a way he recognised from experience with his own soldiers. It was either drink or laudanum that Amelia was addicted to.

Why had Ava kept her on? The girl couldn't possibly be reliable as an actress. Glancing at Ava, he drew back; she was staring at him with her mouth set, knowing exactly what he was seeing. Henry raised his eyebrows in a challenge and she looked away. But he'd made his point. This was a business, not a centre for supporting the homeless.

Ava turned to hand out plates of cake. 'I believe you've met Walter,' she said. 'He is our male lead actor, along with set designer and choreographer. Without him, The Orchid would have vanished into ruins months ago.'

'And you are — as ever — prone to exaggeration,' Walter said, smiling.

'You have a small cast,' Henry said.

'We have a pool of jobbing actors we draw from when we need help and two lads who help with the sets,' Ava said. 'They're in the kitchen with Cook having their evening meal. The rest of us eat later, but they're young and need to go to their beds after the performance.'

'And of course there is Clarence,' Walter said. 'Our right-hand man.'

Ava smiled, as if pleased by the mention of her fiancé's name, but didn't praise him as she had Walter. Swallowing a mouthful of cake, she put the plate down. 'Do the audience like the play?' she said. 'All I can see from the stage is darkness.'

'I had a peek,' Katie said. 'They didn't look impressed.'

'Are you sure?' She frowned.

'Pretty certain — they threw an apple core at me. I don't think it's their type of thing, Shakespeare, like.'

Ava looked at Henry. 'My father used to put on very successful shows, but we don't get the gentlemen any longer who appreciate such things. This is where we need your help. We have to decide whether to try for a higher class of patrons by putting on new and modern plays, or move into musical hall bawdy songs.'

'I can flick my skirts with the best of them,' Katie said.

'I'm not doing that,' Daisy said. 'No one sees my bloomers.'

'That's not an area we want to go into,' Henry said. He couldn't bear the thought of Ava and her girls on stage in cheap dresses, performing for jeering men. And this theatre was in the West End, perfectly positioned to gain a higher class of audience.

He put down his mug. 'We need to improve the theatre to attract the moneyed audiences. That means decorating and heating the place. No matter what play you put on, you're never going to get respectable trade until you improve the place sufficiently for men to be comfortable bringing their wives.'

'We haven't got the money,' Ava said.

'I can provide the money. That's what I'm here for.'

'I thought you were going to shut us down?' Walter said.

'Only if you don't increase your takings.'

Henry looked at them in turn. It was important they knew how serious the situation was. Ava might care for them all like a school mistress, but he wasn't going to do the same. It had taken some persuading for him to convince his father that he could make a success of The Orchid, since Felix Scott-Leigh had been intending to shut the place down the moment Mr. Miller had died.

Henry remembered the letter he had picked up from his father's desk, a much blotted and badly written missive, with ink smudges that looked suspiciously like tears. Sitting at the desk, he had read the sad, brave words written by a young girl in mourning as she pleaded for a chance to take over running the theatre that had been her only home.

When his father's footsteps echoed down the hall, Henry had hastily hidden the letter in his pocket. This tragic Miss Miller must have had few dealings with Felix Scott-Leigh if she believed her letter would elicit a sympathetic response.

The study door slammed open and his father had marched in.

'What are you doing in here?' he said.

'Sorting the post,' Henry said coldly. Years of experience had taught him the correct manner to deal with him father. Emotions had to be put aside, and only the hard facts given. 'Mr Miller of The Orchid has died,' he said. 'His daughter wishes to remain *in situ* as manager.'

'I'm not having a woman running a theatre. Pay her off and the rest of the staff. The place is a drain on my finances.'

Henry cleared his throat. 'I could take a trip down and have a look. West End theatres can be very lucrative, and it would give me something to do.'

Felix eyed him, then smiled. 'Excellent idea. Take a train down tomorrow.'

Henry stared at his father. It had been such a long time since he had met with approval that it surprised and concerned him. But a trip to London would get him away from the suffocating, malevolent atmosphere that always hung in the house, and he was desperate for employment. The idle life of a gentleman had never suited him.

3

Ava dropped the pile of bills into a box on her desk, then dropped her head into her hands. They had been spending so little, but the invoices were still mounting, even though she and Clarence hadn't paid themselves yet. Hopefully Henry wouldn't notice that, as he had been adamant that they were both to receive their salary.

Soon Henry would arrive in her office to look through the figures. She glanced at the clock. Henry was a complication she didn't need. Closing her eyes, she pictured his intelligent eyes and set mouth. Not a man to cross; it was clear he was used to being obeyed. Well, The Orchid would be a shock, because she wasn't going to jump to follow his orders and neither would any of her staff. Most of them resented his presence as much as she did. Clarence in particular had been very vocal over the situation.

There was knock on the door and she straightened. 'Yes?' she said.

Henry walked in, wearing his overcoat and hat.

'Is it that cold?' she said.

'Not far off.' He removed his hat. 'I've been out to arrange stabling for my other horses and carriage, since my man has arrived with them.'

'And your groom? Have you arranged stabling for him too?'

'A warm and comfortable inn. I envy him.' Henry sat down.

Ava looked at him. 'Did your valet come too? I have only just realised that you have no servants.'

'I'm used to managing alone. Actually, I prefer it.'

Ava nodded; it was easy to forget that Henry was from a wealthy family. Maybe it would have been simpler to deal with Charles or Jasper, since neither of them had the sharp, all-seeing look that Henry had. He didn't speak that often, but she was certain that nothing escaped his gaze.

Henry tapped his fingers on the desk. 'I want you to put on a different play.'

'But we're scheduled to run with Anthony and Cleopatra for another week.'

'Then you'll be playing to an empty theatre. It's well acted, but not what your patrons want to see. I spoke to some of them last night and they didn't find the play much fun. We need something light and fresh.'

'Shakespeare plays are very popular.'

'People want different things from the theatre now. Mr Dickens's adaptations are successful, but we can't afford him. Wilde is also doing very well, however he is also beyond our purse.'

'So what can we do?'

'Find a newcomer, a bright youngster who writes excellent scripts and is desperate to make a name for himself. You mentioned a comedy when I first arrived here, and I think I know just the one.'

'I suspect you are friends with such a playwright?' She kept her voice level, but her hands clenched. If Henry thought he could use The Orchid as a testing ground for his amateur writer friends, he was very much mistaken. Not when he was playing with the lives and careers of her actors.

'An acquaintance has penned a humorous farce called *Belle Gives a Ball*. It was recommended to me and I think it is worth paying him a visit.'

'Have you read it?'

Henry went still. 'No, I have not.'

'And who will decide if we put on this play written by your friend?'

Henry rose. 'You will. Now, please fetch your coat and hat and collect a chaperone, whilst I get my carriage.'

He strode out the office and Ava banged her fist against the table. Rude man! Then glancing down at the pile of unpaid bills, she sighed — maybe she did need some help. She was working so hard, she barely had the time to learn her own words, and Henry would have noticed that she'd made two mistakes in last night's performance. Thankfully Clarence had saved her.

Thinking about her assistant manager, Ava frowned. He had changed since their pretend engagement; become more confident around her. Sometimes she wondered if he had forgotten it was only an act. If they were passing in the corridor, he would touch her arm. It was a comfort during this difficult time but sometimes the touch would become a grip and she'd draw back, startled. But she must have been imagining it; her old friend would never hurt her deliberately. In truth, Clarence was her only confidant at The Orchid. Daisy was too young, Katie too wild and Amelia ... well, she had her own problems. Ava sighed, looking at her piled desk. It was lonely being in charge; her fellow actors had been much easier around her before her father had died and she'd become their boss.

Anyway, she'd better fetch her hat

and coat before Henry wondered where she was. Dropping her pen back in the inkwell, she stood up and stretched her back, looking at the faded paint on the walls of the office. Was this to be her life — running a small theatre hand to mouth; dealing with all the problems of her staff and never able to confess her own? But if she didn't carry on, then what would happen to her friends? Clarence and Katie would find other work but Daisy was too shy, Amelia too ill and Walter too old.

Pausing to looking in the mirror that hung behind the door, Ava thrust hatpins through her small felt bonnet. The face staring back was pale, with large shadows deep beneath her eyes; she'd have to layer on the make-up tonight to become the sparkling Queen Cleopatra. Touching the skin around her eyes, she noticed a faint trace of lines. Age had crept up on her as it had on the original Nile queen. Maybe she should marry Clarence for real? It would secure her standing in the theatre world. He had never hidden his regard for her, and it was unlikely that, at almost thirty, any other man would want her.

Opening the door she went down to the kitchen, where Cook stood stirring a pot on the range and Daisy peeled a large basin of onions. The girl looked up through her tears.

'Leave those onions,' Ava said. 'I need your company.'

'Are you going to the shops?'

'No, we are taking a carriage to a friend of Mr Scott-Leigh's home. He's written a script we are to look at.'

'A carriage?' Daisy's eyes widened. 'Or do you mean a hansom cab?'

'A private carriage. Fetch your hat and coat. And wash those hands, else the vehicle will stink like a pickling factory.'

Daisy scuttled over to the sink in the corner of the room, then raced past her and out the door. Ava shook her head. The poor girl was probably terrified, since she'd few dealings with the higher classes. It was probably time she did, else Daisy would be so over-awed when she did meet men of standing she'd be easy prey for those with less than honourable intentions.

Striding back into the hall, Ava remembered that Henry had intended for her to be a servant to his own sister. Not a chance! She'd rather live in a garret and sew for a living than act as a lady's maid, dancing attendance on the whims of another.

Henry was standing in the hall doorway, his black top hat almost touching the ceiling. 'Are you ready?' he said.

She looked up the stairs as Daisy belted down, two steps at once. 'Slow down, girl,' she said. 'You'll break your neck.'

'I didn't want to keep anyone waiting.' Daisy leapt from the last step and landed in the hall, her petticoats lifting to flash white stockings.

Henry quickly looked away and Ava smiled. At least he wasn't a letch, though; she'd take an honourable man any day over one that couldn't keep his hands to himself. His brother Jasper had assumed that since his family owned the theatre, he also owned the girls who worked there. When he visited, Ava had to put mattresses down on her own bedroom floor for the girls to sleep on to keep them safe.

'Ready?' Henry said, then extended his arm to her.

* * *

In the street outside waited a double brougham carriage, with its driver wrapped up in a thick coat. Steam rose from the horses' mouths into the vivid blue winter sky. Ava shivered and pulled her crimson wool wrap closer about her shoulders as the icy air stung her cheeks and snowflakes landed on her sleeve.

'The innkeeper has put hot bricks in the coach,' Henry said.

'Thank you, that's kind,' she said, and the heat rose to her cheeks. She hadn't been so thoughtful of his comfort when she'd put him in a cold bedroom.

Climbing into the coach, she sat down and stretched out her feet to reach the flannel-wrapped bricks on the floor. Daisy scrambled in beside her, mouth open.

'I've never been in a private coach before,' she said. 'It's lovely! Look, these seats bounce and it doesn't smell of wee.'

'I should hope not,' Henry said.

He pulled the door shut behind and reached up to knock on the roof. The driver shouted to his horses, the carriage jerked, and with a rumble of wheels started down the road. Ava shivered at the draught from around the doorframes and picked up one of the bricks to put on her lap.

'Do you want a blanket?' Henry said.

She shook her head and looked out the window to avoid meeting his eyes. Henry appeared bigger inside the tiny carriage, his long legs hunched up towards his chest. In the reflection of the glass, Ava noticed him wince and shift position and remembered his injuries.

'Are you all right?' she said.

'I'm fine, thank you. Are you warm enough?'

The brick was hot on her lap, warming her thighs. 'I am, yes. How far do we have to go?'

'The journey will take us about fifteen minutes. Mr Richards lives in the Strand. He used to work as a journalist for *The Times* newspaper before he became a playwright.'

'And where has his work been shown?'

'In local theatres mostly, although I saw one play performed in a private showing for the Queen, and it was excellent.'

Ava nodded. So Henry had been invited to the palace to watch a play with royalty. She'd always assumed the Scott-Leigh family to be just a few steps above trade, but it appeared she was wrong. 'Have you helped with many of the businesses owned by your family?' she said.

'This is the first time I have worked in business. I joined at army at seventeen.'

'Did you like the army?'

'It suited me. I prefer action to sitting behind a desk. I am not a man who likes the feel of a quill in his hand.'

She jerked back in her seat. It hadn't occurred to her that he was less than happy with his role. He'd hidden his displeasure well.

'Then hopefully you won't need to be here for long,' she said.

His lip curled and Ava lowered her gaze to the floor. She had sounded rude. Even though she didn't want him here, it couldn't be denied that Henry had been only courteous towards her and her staff.

He moistened his lips. 'I have been invalided out of the army. I cannot return.'

'Can you live as a gentleman?'

'As a man with no gainful employment? No, I could not. Snooker halls and taverns bore me. I hunt, but it doesn't obsess me, and I make a poor dinner guest. A person needs a purpose in life.'

'And you have one now?'

His gaze flicked across her. 'I have to make your theatre profitable, however much you resent my presence. Since we work towards the same aim, it would be better if we could be friends.'

Ava turned her head away and stared out the window. He was right of course, but The Orchid was hers and she didn't want his help. Or did she? Since his arrival she'd stopped shivering in her cold room at night, rigid with the fear that creditors were about to arrive at her door. The theatre and its actors were no longer her sole responsibility.

Daisy coughed and Ava looked at where the girl huddled quietly in the corner of the carriage. She must watch what she said, else Daisy would worry. She knew, more than Ava, to fear the debtors' prison because she had grown up in one when her father had been incarcerated. Occasionally she talked of the iron gates covered with blood-red rust, the bullying and starvation. A friend of the family had rescued her, but there would be no one to save Ava.

Pulling her scarf tighter, Ava gazed out the window at the white pavements laced in frost and puffs of soft snow. Lanterns glowed in the dim morning light and the smog cast halos of light around the shop fronts. The carriage passed a butcher's shop, the window stuffed full with hanging geese, their plucked flesh seeming to quiver under the breeze. Would Henry still be here at Christmas time?

Glancing at his stern expression, she smiled cautiously. He could not always have been so dour. Once he must have been a young boy full of life and excitement, rather than the silent man who sat opposite. What had happened to him? Henry's gaze caught hers and she drew a sharp breath as his eyes stared deep into hers, filling her with warmth similar to the hot brick on her lap.

Twisting her head away, Ava kept her gaze on the floorboards until the carriage came to an abrupt stop, her cheeks burning. How could she react in such an embarrassing way to so unsuitable a man? They had to work together in a professional and civil manner.

'We're here,' Henry said, opening the window to lower the door and flicking down the steps. Ava glanced at the startled face of the coachman, who'd climbed down to perform the task. Henry had been right when he said he liked to do things for himself. If it wasn't that protocol demanded it, she was certain he would have driven them here himself.

'Take my arm,' he said to Daisy, who was struggling to climb out onto the compacted ice.

'Thank you,' she said, her breath puffing into the air.

Henry held out his other arm to Ava but she hesitated, fearing his touch. What was wrong with her? This man was well above her station. They had nothing in common. He would marry someone from a similar background as arranged by his family, likely a young girl who was quiet and meek.

And why was she thinking about marriage?

'Ava?' Henry said. 'Daisy's getting cold.'

'Sorry.' She stepped out and his hand gripped her arm as he swung her down onto the pavement.

'We won't be long,' Henry said to the coachman. 'Take the horses around the block to keep them moving.'

'Yes, sir.' The man dipped his head and climbed back up onto his box.

Ava looked at the building in front of them. It was a town house with a red painted door and two burning gas lights. A narrow window box lay filled with snow, and through the glass a fire could be seen burning brightly. This Mr

Sidney Richards might be a new playwright, but he was certainly not short of money.

Henry knocked on the door with the top of his silver-capped cane and a maid opened it.

'Mr Richards, please. He is expecting us,' Henry said.

4

Ava stepped into the house, her arm aching as Daisy clutched it. She'd chosen the wrong companion for this trip. Katie would have been bouncing ahead with curls jumping and a grin on her face. But then again, Katie would also have reported the visit back to everyone at The Orchid, whereas Ava knew that Daisy would keep quiet. It wasn't fair to get everyone's hopes up if the new play came to nothing.

Wiping her slush-covered shoes on the mat, Ava walked into the house and unfastened her coat as a blast of hot air warmed her cheeks. Glancing down, she smiled — the carpet in the hall would have cost more than all her own furniture put together.

A white-capped maid showed them into the parlour. Ava went straight to the fire and held her numb hands out, flexing the fingers as pain spread through her joints. There was a rattle behind her and she turned to see a second girl place a tray holding a tea service and fruit cake on a small table. Her stomach rumbled. After seeing the stack of bills in the post, she hadn't been able to eat her breakfast that morning.

'Sit down, Daisy,' she said, lowering herself into a chair beside the fire. If she was going to be treated like a lady, she would act like one.

A man strode in the door. Aged about twenty-five, he was dressed in the vivid layered clothes of a dandy, and Ava's mouth tightened until she noticed his eyes gleamed bright and intelligent, like a terrier dog's.

'Sidney!' Henry said, shaking hands with the newcomer.

Ava narrowed her eyes at the use of first name terms. Was Henry using The Orchid as a favour for a friend?

'This is Miss Miller,' Henry said,

indicating her. 'And an actress from the theatre, Daisy.'

'Lovely to meet you all,' Sidney said, shaking hands. 'I've heard of you, Miss Miller. One of our few women manageresses.'

Ava narrowed her eyes. Was he about to disapprove of her as well? But Sidney didn't look bothered, smiling at her with an enthusiasm that she couldn't help but warm to.

'I'll get the script,' Sidney said. 'You can't make any decisions until you've read it.'

He vanished from the room and Ava glanced at Henry, raising her eyebrows. 'What did you tell him?' she said.

'That you might be interested in his play. I've known Sidney for several years, but that doesn't mean I'd persuade you to take on a script you weren't happy with. It's your decision.'

Ava nodded, glancing at the door as Sidney raced back with two bound piles of paper. He held one out to her and the second to Henry.

66

'That's all right, I've already seen it performed,' Henry said. 'Pass it over to Daisy, since she's one of the principal actresses.' The girl flushed and reached out to take the script.

Ava opened her copy and scanned the list of characters, then smiled. They would fit the cast of The Orchid well. The play opened with an argument between Belle and her papa, humorously written and reminding her of disagreements with her own father. Next there was a corridor scene — excellent, as it would give them time to change the backdrop for the later ride out in the park and conversation with Belle's mother. It wasn't the most original play she'd ever read, but neither was it mawkish. Henry was right, it would certainly sell.

Pages rustled beside her and she looked at Daisy. The girl was intently studying the words, her brow creased, but she looked up and gave a small nod.

'I like it,' Ava said. 'Have you any other offers?'

'Not yet, but I haven't taken it to many places yet.'

Ava smiled. Sidney was sharp; he wouldn't let his work go for a couple of sovereigns and a kiss. She put the papers down. 'Since you're a new playwright and your name won't be a draw yet, I'm willing to offer you a percentage of profit.'

'How much?'

'Five per cent of net takings.'

'That's hardly fair. I would like five per cent gross, or fifteen per cent net.'

'All right, fifteen per cent net.' She shook his hand. 'And we reserve the right to end the run early if it's not successful.'

'I'm sure it will be, as I'll get my friends to come and see it.'

Ava smiled. For that privilege she would have offered twenty per cent!

'Thank you. It's the perfect play for The Orchid and I hope we can work together to make it a success.'

'Excellent,' Henry said, shaking Sidney's hand. 'We will make arrangements to get the theatre ready. Time to go, ladies.'

'So soon?' Daisy said, looking at the cake.

'Mr Scott-Leigh is right. There is a lot to be done if we're to start this play next week,' Ava said.

'Next week?' Sidney said.

'Of course.' Pulling on her gloves, Ava dipped a brief curtsey and strode to the front door. The quicker they left, the less time it gave Sidney to change his mind. It really was a great little play and she knew several theatres that would have put it on for a substantial cash fee.

The maid opened the front door and Ava stepped through, then paused and looked down at the script she had retained. Did they have the money to improve The Orchid? If this show wasn't successful, she risked them getting further into debt, and there weren't that many pounds between her and Marshalsea prison as it was. But if she didn't take a risk, she would certainly lose the theatre.

Henry touched her arm. 'The carriage is returning. Watch out for the wheels.'

She stepped backwards, then turned her head as the vehicle sent a spray of muddy slush onto her coat. It would be a cold ride home since the hot bricks would have chilled now.

Henry opened the carriage door and she climbed in. A brick sat on her seat and she reached out to move it so she could sit down. Heat burned into her palm and she jumped back with a cry.

Henry looked in the door. 'The coachman says to warn you he has warmed the bricks up at an inn.'

'I thank him,' she said, rubbing her hands briefly before using a fold of her coat to push the flannel-covered brick onto the floor. Luckily she hadn't just sat straight down, else she'd have had burns in a place she wouldn't have liked to admit to.

'That was fun,' Daisy said. 'And he let me take the script away with me. What part do you think I'll play, Miss Miller?'

'Ava,' she said automatically. 'And I'm not sure. Maybe Belle? You look more innocent than Katie.'

Daisy giggled. 'She's not innocent at all. Walking out with a coachman, she is. I've seen them.'

'Is she?' Ava stared at her. She'd been distracted recently, but she should have noticed that. When she got back she'd have a word with Katie and find out what was going on. Katie had always been a flirt, but to her knowledge had never overstepped the bounds of decency. Now if it has been Amelia linked to a coachman she wouldn't have been surprised — that girl was anyone's for half a beer and a pint of prawns.

'So you liked the play?' Henry said.

Ava jumped, then cursed to herself. Why did he make her so feel so

71

nervous? 'Yes, I did,' she said. 'You were right, it's perfect for the Orchid. Can we afford to improve the auditorium though? I have no money.'

'I'm going to cover the costs for now, until the theatre is up to the right standard.'

'Thank you, I appreciate it.' Her shoulders relaxed. Life should be easier with Henry here to help her, but in truth she felt more tense then she had done for months. What was it about him that left her stumbling over her words? Henry was a son of the Scott-Leigh family; she had to get control of herself. He would never be interested in an actress, and if she let her feelings show she'd risk making a fool of herself.

Henry touched her arm and she jumped. 'You shouldn't have to pay for everything,' he said. 'The theatre belongs to my family and the major repair bills should be paid by us. I'm surprised your father didn't explain that to you.'

'We've always saved to pay for renovations out of our share of the profits.'

'And since my family are sharing the profits, we also need to share the cost of major repairs.'

Ava brightened. 'In that case, I've got a large pile of bills at home you can contribute to.'

'I have a feeling I might regret this conversation.' Henry grinned.

Ava smiled and looked out the window at the brightly coloured figures sliding around on the frozen river edge. 'That looks fun. I used to skate here with my father.'

'I can stop the carriage,' Henry offered.

She glanced at him, surprised. He didn't seem the type of person who would enjoy a slide on the ice. Looking back out the window again, she nodded. It would be nice to have some fun, and the excitement of getting the script had lifted her spirits.

'All right,' she said. 'There's a verge

ahead we could stop on.'

'I'm staying in here,' Daisy said. 'My boots are holed enough. Any more damage and I'll only be wearing me uppers!'

Ava climbed down the steps onto the crunchy grass, the freezing air filling her lungs. In front of her the ice stretched across the river to the other side of the bank, glinting in the winter sunshine. Clad in bright coats, a group of children slid across, yelling and laughing. Then with a thud, a girl in a red shawl squealed as she landed on her bottom.

'It doesn't look very dignified,' Ava said.

'Perhaps you'd better take my arm?' Henry said.

She glanced at it, remembering her reaction to his touch earlier. Honestly, she was worse than Daisy when the post boy spoke to her. It must be because Henry made her feel safe, and it helped to have someone to share her worries over The Orchid with. They were both on the same side at work, but she would have to be careful because she couldn't trust him completely. He would sell the theatre if it couldn't be made profitable.

Ava breathed in sweet-smelling hot smoke from the chestnut stalls that lined the frozen river bank. Kiosks were hiring skates, but for a brief slide her boots would be more than adequate. Her shoulders relaxed and she smiled; it had been a while since she had had fun. Life had been about work for such a long time now. Smiling, she took Henry's arm.

'Tread carefully,' he said, putting his cane on the grass.

She stopped. 'Is this a good idea? What if you fall?'

'I think I'll survive, madam. After travelling back from the East wrapped in bandages and chewing a leather strip for pain relief, I doubt the Thames will kill me.'

Ava winced. 'What happened to you?' she said, then bit her lip. It was a very personal question, and so far he'd been reserved.

Henry stepped onto the ice, pushing down with his boot to check it was safe. Nodding, he reached up to help her down beside him. 'I was shot twice,' he said. 'In the face and my back.'

She inhaled sharply. 'You were lucky to survive.' Picturing him lying covered in blood on a battlefield, she shuddered. How terrible it was that he had suffered.

'Modern medicine saved me, and a brilliant young army doctor. It is fine now, and there were plenty wounded worse than I.'

Ava doubted it, but reached out her arm. It wasn't fair to push him to talk about it when he'd clearly rather not.

'Ready?' He tested the ice again. 'It's quite thick.'

She clutched him as he kicked forwards and they shot across the ice, a cold breeze against her cheeks. The ice slid under her boots, making her wobble and, laughing, she pushed back with her foot to propel them faster. Henry was more nimble than she expected. His arm gripping her, he guided her away from the thinner ice in the centre of the river, and she grinned as they shot back across the frozen water.

Her father had often slid with her here and her smile faded as she remembered him beside her, holding her arm in the way Henry now did. It had been such a short illness that carried Papa off, she hardly had the chance to say goodbye. Even now, when she returned to the theatre, she expected to see his hat hanging in the hall. She shivered, tears pricking her eyes. What would he say if he could see the mess she had made of his theatre?

Actually, she knew what he'd say. He would put his arm around her and tell her that it would all be all right. That he would take care of it. But then, relying on him had been part of the problem — she hadn't taken responsibility for The Orchid whilst he was still alive.

And now, without that essential business training, she was drowning in debt.

'Are you cold?' Henry said, stopping.

'No, I was just thinking about my father. How he loved sliding on the ice in winter.'

'You must miss him.'

She nodded, swallowing as a hard lump gathered in her throat.

'Do you have any other family?' he said.

'None. My mother left when I was a baby — she was an actress at the theatre and not prepared to sacrifice her career for a child.' Raising her chin, she looked directly at him. 'They weren't married.'

'I know.'

'I'm surprised, with your concern over morality, that your family let us stay.'

'Your father was discreet and theatres have never been the most upstanding of places. You wouldn't have got away with it in one of our other businesses.'

'So we would have been sent out

78

onto the streets?'

He looked at her directly. 'My father would have ordered you out. He is a man to be careful of, I warn you. The only thing he cares about is money; even his family comes in second place.'

'I suppose it is business. You have said you will shut us down if we do not turn a profit.'

'But not turn you all onto the streets. I would find you other situations. I am not my father, Miss Miller.'

Luckily her cheeks were already warm from skating, else he'd have seen her flush. It was true she had thought him harder than he was. 'I suspect I have been reading too many of Mr Dickens's books,' she said with a short laugh.

'Not all managers are the same. You care for your staff, don't you?' he said.

'Yes; they are like my family. That is why I am so desperate for us to survive, else we will be parted. We each have little family and few friends.'

'Maybe I could settle them on the

estate if we can't make The Orchid profitable?'

'A life in service wouldn't suit them any more then it would me. There is no freedom in service.'

'I suspect it is better than starving.'

She looked back at the carriage waiting by the side of the river. 'This morning was the first time Daisy had ever been in a private carriage,' she said.

'Ava.'

He took hold of her hands and the warmth — even through her gloves — made her jump. 'Ava, I can't provide carriage rides, food and housing to everyone in London. I am a man of means, but I don't have enough to save everyone. I know you want to protect your friends, but they're adults and also responsible for their own lives. It is impossible for you to care for everyone.'

'I know.' She pulled her hands away. 'But my staff work hard, and during the difficult times they worked for bed and board because they knew I couldn't afford to pay them. It would be wrong of me to turn them out onto the street.'

'Let's not talk about turning people onto the street. We're going to make a success of this theatre. True, it needs investment and work, but it's in a good position and had a good reputation once. The Orchid can be brought back to its former glory, I am certain. It will just take time.'

'How long are you going to give us?'

'Until I am certain it cannot be saved. You must work with me though, rather than resenting my presence.'

'I don't.'

'I think you do. I would, in your situation. I resented the officer who took over my men after I was injured and discharged from the army. I don't think your situation is so very different. You were used to having complete control; then a complete stranger arrived to take over.'

'We needed help.' Ava stared at the floor. 'I thought I could run the place, but tradesmen won't give me the rates they used to. I am scared of what will happen to us all if I fail. What else can I do? I am alone in the world.'

'But you are engaged to Clarence.' He frowned.

Ava caught her breath and stepped back. She couldn't lie to this man who was doing his best to help her. 'I am not marrying Clarence.'

'You have broken it off? I am shocked. He did not look sad when I saw him this morning.'

'It was an engagement we rushed into,' she said. It was at least partly true.

'So you are a free woman again?'

Twisting her gaze away, she went hot, then cold. This was Henry Scott-Leigh, a man well above her station. She was theatre scum, an immoral lady.

'Ava?' he said, his voice gentle.

Draw by the warmth in his tones, she stared directly into his dark brown eyes, which were almost black under the pale winter light. His scar twisted his face, but she hardly noticed as his fingers tightened on hers. Then he tilted his head to touch his lips to hers, stubble grazing her cheeks.

Ava thrust him backwards, breathing sharply.

He grabbed her arm. 'Wait, Ava — don't run.'

'Let go of me!' She twisted away from him. What on earth had Henry been thinking of? He had seemed so principled. What could possess him to act in such an outlandish way? Even married couples didn't behave in that manner in public. Her reputation would be in ruins if they had been noticed, and it was bad enough already.

Her feet sliding on the ice, she scrambled onto the bank, breath coming out in clouds as she raced for the coach. How dare he do that! She was no cheap girl who'd act as his mistress. Was that what he thought? That along with the theatre, he owned her?

'Ava, stop,' Henry said, and he grasped her arm, pulling her around to face him. 'I'm sorry. I don't know why I did that.'

'Neither do I.'

'Actually, I do know. You looked so beautiful standing in front of me, with your glorious hair and flushed cheeks.'

'And you were unable to resist? I've heard that rubbish before, Mr Scott-Leigh, from men more powerful than yourself. I didn't believe them either.'

Henry took a step backwards. 'I just know that despite your birth and social rank, and even the job you do, I'm drawn to you in a way I have never been to another woman.'

Her mouth dropped open. 'I don't think I want to hear that opinion of me. And just in case you're in doubt, let me make myself plain. I would not ever become any man's hired girl, not even if it meant keeping The Orchid. If you think that I come along with the threadbare seats and rickety stage, then you are very much mistaken.'

'I thought you were engaged and therefore completely out of bounds.

When you told me you weren't, I was so relieved I acted on impulse.'

'I am still out of bounds. You, Mr Scott-Leigh, have looked down on me and my workers since your arrival. Yes, we are in a trade which has a reputation for wanton behaviour, but that doesn't mean we are folk with poor morals. Daisy there, sat waiting quietly in the cold carriage, has never even been kissed, and despite their fluttering and chaperones, I doubt that's a claim many of the girls of your rank could claim at the age of twenty. We're decent people.'

'I'm not suggesting you become my mistress,' he said, his voice hard. 'Since when did I ask that?'

'What are you saying then?'

'Nothing! Just that I like you. The kiss was an impulse, and one I am now heartily regretting. I suggest we forget this whole thing and remain the strict business partners that we're supposed to be.'

'Yes, I think we should. This will

never be mentioned again, and certainly, you do not have leave to ever kiss me again.'

'Rest assured, madam, I will never be tempted to do so again.' Turning, he strode back to the carriage.

Feet freezing in the snow, Ava watched him go. She had reacted so violently because she had desired the kiss so much. But it could go no further. Henry-Scott Leigh could never be anything to her; their backgrounds were too diverse. He would never accept her as the person she was — a woman who worked for a living and lived a life far different from his own.

5

Henry tied his cravat, then sighed as someone knocked on his door; he'd have preferred to remain undisturbed this morning. Yesterday had been uncomfortable, even though Ava had shut herself in her office as soon as they'd returned. With slight trepidation, he had explained to the staff that they needed to learn a new play in a week, but to his relief — except for Clarence — they had been enthusiastic. Borrowing the script from Daisy, Walter and the girls had held an impromptu rehearsal. Henry would have enjoyed it if he hadn't been so aware of Ava alone in her study. Why had he kissed her? Such a foolish thing to do. She would now think him no better than his brothers.

There was a second knock on the door and he glanced up. 'Come in.'

'Hello,' Walter said, opening it. 'Wasn't sure if you'd heard me.'

'Just getting dressed; you're up early.'

'We're excited about this new play. Do you think it will save us?'

Henry looked at Walter; noticing in the pale morning night faint lines tracing down from his nose and across his eyes. The man's cheeks were sunken and pale. No matter how often Ava reassured them, all the staff knew that the theatre was nearly bankrupt. If The Orchid was to close down, they would lose their home and livelihoods. How easy would it be for a man like Walter to find work? Would he end his days sweeping the streets or mending chairs like so many of his fellow ageing thespians?

'Is Miss Miller up?' Henry said.

'Ava is in her office sorting through the post. She asked me to come and tell you to pack your bags.'

'Pack my bags?' Henry echoed, startled. Had she thrown him out?

Walter grinned. 'The mistress has

prepared the room at the top of the stairs for you. It's larger and warmer.'

'That's very kind of her.' Henry breathed deeply, relaxing his shoulders. He couldn't leave now, not when it would mean never seeing her again.

Then he shook his head. What *was* he thinking? What did it matter if he never saw her again? In fact that would be the best solution, because she was the last person he should ever fall in love with. He remembered Harriet, with her shining eyes and wide smile that she had eagerly bestowed on so many men. He couldn't go through that again.

'Would you like me to help you move?' Walter said.

Henry shook his head — he wasn't going to use Ava's staff as free labour.

'I'll do it later, but thank you. This room was a little uncomfortable.'

Walter nodded, smiling as he left, which confirmed Henry's suspicions that he'd been put in the room deliberately. What had changed Ava's mind? It certainly couldn't have been the kiss. Maybe it was because she thought he would save The Orchid? Leaning down to pull on his boots, he touched the threadbare carpet and grimaced. The play was a nice, funny little piece, but the theatre was so run-down it needed months of work doing and hundreds of pounds spending on it. Why it had been left to get into such a state, he didn't know. What had Ava's father been thinking?

He took a deep breath and strode out onto the landing. What would it be like when he met Ava this morning? She wasn't the type to blush and hide her face. In fact, he'd got off quite lightly yesterday; it had been the surprise element, probably. It had been so nice skating with her — holding her hand and talking in an easy way he'd not done with any woman since Harriet. Well, he wasn't going to dwell on his mistake. He'd apologised, and Ava wasn't the sort of woman who'd make a long-running fuss about such a thing.

Loud voices and laughter flooded from the small parlour used as a breakfast room. Walter had been right when he'd said everyone had got up early. Walking in the door, Henry glanced at the platter of bacon and eggs on the table; buttered toast stood on a hot-water plate, along with pots of sticky strawberry jam. Ava must have told Cook to prepare a feast. He'd gotten used to the two slices of toast and a scrape of conserve that was the usual breakfast at The Orchid. Shame that on the one day they had a proper breakfast, he didn't feel hungry at all.

'Here's a space,' Daisy said, shuffling her chair sideways.

Henry pulled out the seat and sat down. Up to now none of the cast had been very friendly, except for Walter, who he suspected would be decent to a pickpocket. It was amazing the difference now they thought he would save them from the workhouse.

The door opened again and Ava walked in, her brow creased and lips pressed tight. Whatever she'd found in the post clearly hadn't cheered her up. Neither would the fact that the only seat left free was beside him. She glanced at it and frowned, smoothing down her dark-print work gown as she sat beside him. At least there would be no talk of yesterday's indiscretion while all her staff were around the table. Though since Daisy had been in the carriage while they'd skated, it was quite possible they already knew.

'Tea?' Ava said.

'Please,' he answered, putting his cup down beside her.

'Lemon, isn't it?'

He nodded, pleased that she had remembered. Taking the mug back, his fingers brushed hers and he spilled tea onto the white cloth.

'Butterfingers,' Daisy said, helping herself to more toast. 'Do you want some more scrambled egg, Katie?'

'No thanks,' Katie said, her voice flat.

Henry looked at her; the girl's normally cheerful face was pale and her eyes were surrounded by thick black shadows. Ava must have noticed too, because she said, 'I saw you hanging about outside the theatre last night, Katie. I don't expect that type of behaviour from my girls.'

'Sorry.'

'What were you doing?'

'Nothing.'

'Katie?'

The girl drew in a sharp breath before flinging her head down on the tablecloth with a dramatic cry. Henry stifled a smile; she truly was a born actress.

'I wanted to see David,' Katie said, her voice muffled.

'Well, you shouldn't have been seeing him at all. That's the behaviour of a slapper, not a respectable actress.'

'He did respect me. He said he wanted to marry me!'

Ava dropped her knife. 'And what did you say?'

'I said yes. I love him.' Katie threw her head back onto the table and broke into loud sobs.

'For someone who's just got engaged, you don't look that happy,' Walter said, patting her on the shoulder.

'Because he doesn't want to marry me anymore!'

'Take the butter out from under her head,' Ava said, 'else we'll get nits in our lunchtime sandwiches.'

'I haven't got nits!'

'No, I'm sure you haven't. Just put it over there, Daisy. Now, Katie, this boy said he didn't want to marry you anymore. Did he say why?'

'He's going with Rosie from the butcher's shop, because she gets him free off-cuts of beef.'

'Then I think you should value yourself more,' Ava said briskly. 'A brilliant, up-and-coming young actress with a marvellous future ahead, compared to a bit of free stewing steak?

94

When you're starring at Drury Lane you can wave at them sitting in their cheap seats.'

Katie smiled through her tears. 'But I don't want to work at Drury Lane. I want to stay here.'

'Which you will, as long as you stop sneaking out to meet boys.' Ava reached out to squeeze her hand. 'No man is going to wed you for something you're giving away free. Have more dignity and the next time you meet a young chap, invite him to join us for tea in the parlour so he can meet all of us. If he comes back after that, you know you've got a keeper.'

'Meet everyone? Then I'm going to die a spinster.' She collapsed again. 'I didn't really like him that much anyway, but with the theatre going bankrupt I thought he was a better option than the workhouse.'

'That's no reason to wed someone.'

'You won't end up in the workhouse. I will find you a place if it comes to that,' Henry said. 'My family have businesses all over London.'

'Not in a factory? I've seen them,' Katie said.

'We don't own any factories. We have restaurants, theatres and music halls.'

'Amelia could work in your music hall. Great voice she has,' said Katie.

Henry glanced down the table at where Amelia hid behind the teapot. With sallow, yellowish skin and thin hair, she looked older than her years. He knew from Ava that she was only about eighteen, but the gin had destroyed her looks and he suspected she would be lucky to reach the summer.

'What improvements are you thinking of making to the theatre?' Walter said, putting his knife and fork down.

'I'm going to have a walk around today and decide. Whatever we choose to do, it must be done fast.'

'We?' Clarence said from the door. 'I didn't know there was a 'we' involved. I thought you were just going to tell us what to do.'

Henry breathed deeply. He mustn't rise to it, since that was what Clarence wanted. Instead he should show patience with the assistant manager, who would be mourning the loss of Ava. She might believe the split was amicable, but he'd seen Clarence staring at her last night with his eyes narrowed and filled with longing.

'I've not run a theatre before,' Henry said. 'So I want everyone's input.'

'We need to improve the seats,' Daisy said. 'I sat on one last week during rehearsal and got stabbed in the arse by a spring.'

'Bottom, please, Daisy,' Ava said.

'The seats are dreadful,' Walter said. 'And the damp. The walls are mouldy and the curtains are covered in mildew. We need to get the place dried out and more fires lit, else any new paint will peel straight off.'

'More fires! Great, I'm all for them,' Katie said. 'Daisy and I sleep in our overcoats.'

'Coal is so expensive and this is such

a large building,' Ava said.

'Just order it,' Henry said. 'I'll take care of the bill. Walter's right; we have to get this place warm. If it's like this in November, what will be like in December? And you will want to attract the lucrative Christmas trade.'

'How do you know what is best to do when you haven't worked in a theatre before?' Clarence said.

'Because I've been speaking to the managers of other theatres. It's only a few weeks until Christmas and by then I expect The Orchid to be showing some success, so I can head back home.'

'You'll be leaving us?' Daisy said.

'I'm not the manager; that's Ava.'

Ava looked at him quickly and he smiled. He still wasn't sure about a female manageress, but it couldn't be denied that she knew both her actors and the theatre. It was the finances and management of a large and old building she found difficult, and he could teach her that. It was the training of actors and organising rehearsals he couldn't do. The army had taught him common sense and how to organise people and equipment, but deciding what corset Daisy should wear was completely beyond him.

'We'll all do the walk around,' Ava said. 'It's important everyone is involved.'

'I have paperwork to do,' Clarence said.

'I'm sure it can wait half an hour.' The assistant manager's mouth twitched.

'I'm not sure . . . ' Amelia said, sitting up.

'Everyone,' Ava said, her voice firm. 'You can go out later for your daily walk, but for the moment The Orchid needs you.'

'I won't be much help.' The young girl stared at her feet.

'You have a wonderful voice and in this new play there is an ideal spot for you. But I need to be able to rely on you.' Ava looked at the girl.

Again examining Amelia's pale face,

Henry was more inclined to wonder if she would survive until the end of the play run, let alone until the summer. It was surprising that Ava kept on a girl with such obvious problems. Whilst commendable from an altruistic point of view, it wasn't the way to run a business.

Pushing back his chair, he rose. 'Has everyone finished?'

6

Ava followed Henry and Walter, a notebook in her hand. It seemed odd to be walking around the theatre under someone else's instruction. The Orchid had always been hers and her father's. Glancing at the corridors her papa used to stride down, she blinked and drew in a deep breath. How she missed his love and support! Now she was on her own in a crumbling playhouse. The place must have been struggling for years — she could see that now — yet her father had kept it from her.

Henry pushed open the doors to the auditorium and Ava shivered, breathing in damp air laced with the scent of mildew. Under bright winter daylight the wallpaper bubbled out into wet patches from the plaster, stained with black mould. Her cheeks flushed. She'd been so intent on saving money, she hadn't realised the damage it was doing. It might be cheaper to run the place with minimum heating and lighting, but who would want to visit?

'Have we got time to clean this up?' she said.

Henry glanced back. 'It's going to be a long process; there have been years of neglect.'

She pressed her lips together. It wasn't nice to hear him criticise her father, even when she was suspecting the same thing. 'How long will you be staying?' she said.

'I'll get the works started, then you can oversee them. I have other businesses I need to concentrate on, too; The Orchid is a fairly small part of our investments.'

Ava nodded. He hadn't sound disappointed to be leaving soon — though to be honest, he couldn't be blamed for that. He was a wealthy man and used to comfort and servants, despite his army background. She'd put him in a cold and miserable room. It was no wonder he couldn't wait to get away.

But the kiss . . . It hadn't felt like the action of a man desperate to get away. Why had he done it? He couldn't be in love with her, since he'd made it clear that he didn't approve of either her or her lifestyle. Oh, what did it matter? Henry was her boss and nothing more. But it had felt so good . . .

'Ava?' Henry said.

She looked up, cheeks warming.

'The renovation?' he said. 'Can you manage it?'

'Yes, of course I can.' But her voice sounded sharp.

'You won't be doing it on your own anyway,' Walter said. 'Would she, Clarence?'

'No,' Clarence said, but his tone was flat and Ava closed her eyes briefly. Pretending he was her fiancé had been a mistake. Clarence hadn't been the same around her since and it wasn't easy to ignore his silences or angry behaviour. It made her feel even lonelier, and her isolation would only get worse when Henry returned home. Sighing, she wrapped her shawl closer to her shoulders for comfort.

'In the entrance hall I thought we could sell chestnuts and boxes of chocolates,' Henry said.

'The hawkers sell those outside,' Clarence said. 'They won't be too happy if they lose their trade.'

'I need to get rid of the hawkers. At the moment our visitors are being harassed by hot chestnut sellers and matchstick girls in rags. As sorry as I am for these unfortunates, if we're not careful we'll all be out there with baskets.'

'We might be,' Katie said. 'I doubt you will be, though.'

He ignored her. 'I've spoken to Cook and she's going to prepare baskets of hot nuts to sell. The ticket sellers can man the stall.'

Walter nodded. 'That's a good idea, and we could order wholesale boxes of chocolates to sell too, and bags of boiled sweets for the cheap seats.'

'They won't make much money,' Ava said.

'The plan isn't to make money, it's to make the theatre more desirable to visit,' Henry said. 'We need to improve the bar area with tables and seats for the ladies. Theatre bars have a reputation for higher prices, so the patrons will accept it and be prepared to pay a premium for a glass of wine — but it's got to be good wine. No cheap stuff.'

Ava nodded, picturing what Henry said in her mind. Could they really make The Orchid work in the way Henry believed? She'd be proud to be its manageress then; could hold her head up high amongst the other theatre owners. Desperate to make money, she'd lowered both prices and standards, but she could see now that that had been the wrong move to make. The Orchid was in the West End, perfectly situated for the moneyed crowd.

She held out her pencil and notebook. 'Jot down what we need to do.'

Henry stepped back. 'Why don't you do it?'

Flushing, she turned away from him. What a fuss! She was only trying to be helpful, not giving him the key to her room or something. Opening the book, she wrote down his suggestions. 'Is that everything?' she said, holding up the page.

'What about the set for the new play?' Walter said.

'I'll employ a couple of joiners,' Henry said. 'We need something dramatic, especially for the ballroom scene.'

Ava snapped her book shut. When had Henry become an expert on putting on a play? Until last week he'd never been involved in running a theatre. Just because he had money, he seemed to think he could take over completely. Looking up, she saw a sarcastic smile on Clarence's face and smiled at him. Poor Clarence. She had been neglecting him recently.

Stepping forward, Clarence squeezed

her hand, his fingers hard against the soft flesh.

'You're looking tired,' he said. 'Didn't you sleep well?'

She hadn't — thoughts of Henry had filled her mind, and memories of his lips on hers. There was no way she could tell Clarence that though. 'I'm fine,' she said. 'There's a lot to do, that's all.'

'I'll come to your office afterwards and we can go through it.'

She nodded. Dear Clarence. If he had felt snubbed by her behaviour these last few days, he wasn't going to hold it against her. He'd been the only person in the theatre she could relax with since the death of her father. All the others, even Walter, treated her differently since she'd become their manageress. Only Clarence had remained the same, cheering her up with jokes and supporting her when the stress became too much.

'If we've finished here,' Ava said, 'I need to go back to my office and start organising the extra actors we need. Katie, could you take the script down to the printers and ask them to make copies for us?'

'Me?' Katie said.

'Yes, of course you. There aren't any other Katies here, are there?'

'I can go for you,' Daisy said. 'I fancy some fresh air.'

Ava frowned but nodded. She'd find something else for Katie to do; the girl had a tendency to be lazy. 'I'll meet you all on the stage at eleven to start going through the script,' she said. Henry looked at her and she smiled back sweetly. It was nice to regain some control over her theatre again. He might know how to do the repairs and make money, but he knew nothing about putting on a play.

* * *

Walter flung Ava's office door open. 'We've sold three quarters of our tickets! Even for the boxes, which I never thought we'd shift.'

'I think you'll find that our playwright and his friends have booked those,' she said. 'What wonderful news though!'

'Henry's done a marvellous job. But I'm glad I wasn't one of those workmen; he can't half yell when he wants to. Scared the woodworm out of the rafters, he did.'

'I suppose that's his army training.' Standing up, she reached for her shawl and wrapped it over her shoulders. The new fires were taking some getting used to. She'd been so used to melting her inkpot over the candle that it had become instinctive. Now she could work in her winter dress and woollen stockings without having to pile blankets over her legs to stop her feet going blue.

But would it last after Henry had returned home? She didn't have enough money to pay the bills without him. She glanced at the calendar and sighed. It wasn't only the money she'd miss, but his support and company. It was probably for the best though. Last night she'd seen him watching her, eyes narrowed, as if trying to find a fault.

Now, flinging a shawl around her head, she checked the mirror, then cursed under her breath at her reddened eyes. Oh, what did it matter what she looked like? She paused, staring into the glass, raising a hand to her mouth. What type of lover would Henry be? She would have guessed awkward until the kiss, which had been filled with experience and passion. There was something burning underneath his controlled exterior — a sensuality that revealed itself in the firm touch of his hand on hers and the expression of desire in his eyes.

'Ava?' Walter said.

She shook her head. Thank goodness Walter couldn't see into her mind. 'Let's go,' she said. 'I have the length of the passageway to turn myself into a lady.'

'You're always a lady.' He took her arm.

She smiled. 'I doubt everyone would agree.'

'In pride, manner and kindness there are few ladies higher than you. I admire you immensely, Ava. There aren't many girls that would have taken on the job of manageress here, and I suspect you only do it to protect the rest of us.'

'I like putting on the plays, and acting. It's the finances I find difficult. My father trained me for the stage and to run a play; he did the book-keeping himself.'

'Hopefully that is where Henry can help us, and even after he leaves I am sure he will stay in contact.'

'As long as we make money.'

'Oh, my dear! I know the situation exactly; there's no need to try and hide it from us. Even Amelia knows that if this play isn't a success, he will shut us down. And where will we all go then? The workhouse for Christmas, I suspect, for addicted Amelia and ancient old me.'

'You're not that old, Walter.'

'Life has hurried past me at The Orchid. I always believed I would marry and have a family of my own, but I can't support one as an actor. I should have left theatre work years ago and trained in something useful, but I love treading those boards too much. This place is my home, this is my family, and there will be none sadder then I should we fail to make it work.'

Ava squeezed his arm. 'I am sure we can bring it back to the state it used to be in when we were visited by earls and dukes. I remember those days — my father in his suit welcoming them in, showing them to their seats. It will happen again, I'm sure.'

'I think your father lost his spirit towards the end.'

'He did.' Ava remembered the pale face on the pillow and the wrinkled hand grasping hers. Papa had been exhausted from years of managing difficult actors and raising a young girl

112

alone. Maybe he'd been lonely, too? There had been no other woman after her mother. Would that be her own fate as well — a life wearied by work and responsibility, with none to share the burden? Should she look for a husband? Henry's face appeared in her mind and she screwed her eyes shut in a bid to blank it out. No, never him!

7

Ava pushed the last comb into Daisy's hair and stepped back. Threaded with pearls, the dark silky strands shone under the gaslight. 'You could hold your head high in any ballroom,' she said.

'Until I speak,' Daisy said, but she raised a hand to touch the curls.

'Where's Katie?'

'Already dressed. She's gone to wait in the wings for the play to start — I reckon she's a bit nervous. This is her biggest part yet.'

'She has been looking a bit pale today; I hope it's not proving too much for her.'

'Katie's delighted to play the lead.' Daisy looked wistfully at the script lying on the table.

'It'll be you next time. I chose Katie this time because after reading the play again I realised she fitted the character better. Belle is a lively, vivacious girl who flirts with the men, but comes home to her mother.'

'Just like Katie then,' Daisy said, grinning. 'Except for the mother, since she hasn't got one of those.'

'I think we make up a family here.' Ava squeezed the girl's shoulder. 'Now if you're done, go and join her while I check on the men.'

'It'll be funny not having you in the play, miss.'

'You won't notice once you get started.'

Ava watched her walk out of the room, her back straight and head high, and smiled. Daisy was already getting into character. Sitting down, she tapped her fingers on the script. She had intended to play the part of Daisy's mother, but at the last moment had handed the part over to an experienced jobbing actress. While she loved acting, and certainly wasn't giving it up, she wondered if appearing on the stage made people doubt her ability to run The Orchid. Until Henry returned home, she would concentrate on working behind the scenes. If she was going to keep her job, she needed to prove to him that she could cope.

Sighing, Ava rubbed a hand over her sore eyes and yawned. Hopefully tonight, if this show was a success, she would be able to sleep. Every night this week she had been kept awake by the churning in her stomach. If the play failed, she and the cast of the theatre would all be out of a job. Henry was a kind man, but he was also a business-man and she had no doubt that if he had to shut the place down, he certainly would do so.

Henry. Closing her eyes, she leant against the cold mirror. He was another reason she couldn't sleep, but instead lay restless in her bed. Why should his image haunt her?

Glancing at the clock, she rose to her feet. At least The Orchid was a more comfortable place to live in now.

116

Confused though she was over Henry, it was undeniable that he'd made great improvements. Sitting in one of the new seats earlier today, she hadn't been able to feel the horsehair stuffed inside the cushion at all, or the smell of damp had gone along with the mouldy curtains. Goodness knew how much it had all cost, but Henry had paid without flinching. It was surprising, since his father and brothers had always been so tight with cash — her own father had had to fight them for every penny. No wonder the place had been so run-down.

Pushing open the door, Ava knocked on the men's dressing-room door. 'Curtain time!' she said.

Walter opened the door, standing in the frame while he knotted his tie. 'All ready, Ava.' His fingers shook as he struggled with the fabric.

'Let me.' Ava deftly fastened it for him. 'And break a leg. It's a big audience, so play them right and we could have a hit on our hands.'

'It's been long time since we had one of those.'

The stage door banged and a man strode quickly up the corridor. Ava glanced down to see Henry, his face flushed red and mouth set. What on earth could be the matter? Surely he wasn't angry because she'd helped Walter with his tie?

'Everything all right?' Walter said.

'No,' Henry said, then glanced at Walter's stage clothes. 'Yes, it's fine. Ava, I need you. Now.'

Ava moistened her lips. She'd never seen Henry looking this anxious, not even when the chimney sweeps had emptied the contents of the flue over the new seat covers in the auditorium. Whirling around, he marched back down the corridor and picking up her skirts, she ran after.

'What is it?' she hissed.

Pushing open the door to the stage, he held it open for her. 'I have to show you something. Katie!' he called. 'Come here.'

There was a rustle of material and Katie put her head around the wings of the stage. Her cheeks gleamed under the gas light and Ava blinked, before realising that the girl's face was drenched in tears. 'Stage fright?' she said.

'No,' Henry said grimly.

Katie stepped stood in front of them, her face bowed.

'Belle is a young innocent maid,' Henry said. 'I'm not sure that's quite the look we're going for.'

Ava stared at Katie, at the beaded hair and demure neckline. The rounded stomach that thrust her gown up high. 'Oh no!' she said, clasping a hand to her mouth. 'Katie! No wonder you wouldn't let me dress you.'

'I'm so sorry,' Katie said, collapsing in tears on her knees. 'I thought I could deal with it. I went to a woman, but I didn't have enough money.'

'Why didn't you come to me?'

'I was so ashamed. And I didn't want to bother you when you were trying to save The Orchid. I didn't want to cause you any more trouble.'

'We can talk about this later,' Henry said. 'But we have curtain up in ten minutes and our virgin heroine is clearly with child. Who is the understudy?'

Ava looked at him. 'Me.'

'Do you know the script?'

'Mostly; the rest of the cast might have to help me out. Katie, you need to change out of that dress; we'll have to hope it fits me.'

The girl shook her head, sobbing. 'I can't move.'

'Yes, you can.' Ava took hold of her hand and yanked her up. 'This is no time for hysterics.'

'But I've ruined everything!'

'I think London will survive the scandal of a pregnant actress,' Henry said. 'I can assure you, it's not the first time it has happened.'

'But we were all trying so hard to be good! Now you'll believe we're cheap girls.' She threw her hands over her face. 'And it's true!'

'I'm not discussing this now. Ava, take her to the dressing room, please, and get changed. You're on stage in less than ten minutes. The curtain has to go up in time else we'll look incompetent before we've even started.'

Ava took Katie's arm and led her off the stage. Katie couldn't have chosen a worse time if she'd tried. After all her insistence to Henry that her girls were well-behaved, she now had to be shown up in such a humiliating way. It reinforced everything he already believed to be true about theatre folk. How could Katie be so foolish? Without that ring on your finger, it was an impulse that could destroy your life.

If only she'd noticed earlier what the girl had been up to. But she'd been so caught up with the new plans for the theatre, and Henry, she hadn't noticed. Katie must have been terrified to have considered going to some backstreet woman! In no way could she let the girl try that again; she'd seen too many women die that way. No, the baby would have to be born and arrangements made.

Racing into the dressing room, Ava yelled for Amelia and turned her back when the startled girl came running down the corridor.

'Unlace me quick,' she said. 'I have to swap dresses with Katie.'

Thankfully, Amelia didn't query it, but merely began to unfasten her gown while Ava grabbed a comb from the dresser and twisted her hair up into a younger style. Hopefully, she would be able to carry off the part of a seventeen-year-old girl.

8

Henry looked up when Ava strode into the parlour with Katie trailing behind her. 'Do you want me to leave?' he said.

Ava shook her head. He might as well know what was happening — and if he disapproved of her solution, then so be it. Henry picked up a paper and stared at it. She shivered; it would have their reviews from last night. There wasn't time now to read them, though. No doubt Henry had already seen them, and he wasn't looking that happy.

Katie sat down on the settle, her face pale, then bowing her head, bunching up the fabric of her print dress with trembling fingers. Henry raised his paper to shield his face and Ava smiled grimly. Dealing with pregnant actresses probably wasn't something he had much experience of. But then neither did she, to be honest. 'How far along are you, Katie?' she said, perching on the edge of a chair.

'I think it's about four months.'

Ava dropped her gaze to the girl's waist, which was hard to see beneath her apron, and sighed. The problems with The Orchid had distracted her from looking after her girls. Since when had Katie worn aprons? It looked like one of Daisy's. Had they been hiding this secret together?

'Who else knows about this?'

'Him! And he didn't want to know.'

'Your . . . ' She had to give the girl some respect. 'Your ex-fiancé? Only he knows?'

Katie sniffed. 'And Amelia. She found me throwing up in the lavvy. I told her it were a stomach bug, but she knew I was lying. She wanted me to tell you, but I thought I could deal with it myself.'

'So you went to see a woman?'

Katie hunched over. 'Please don't report me!'

'Don't be ridiculous, of course I'm

not going to report you. Did this woman touch you at all?'

'I didn't have enough money.'

'You have been a very lucky girl. Do you know how many girls die after visiting places like that?'

'I was desperate.' Wailing, she doubled up.

'Calm down; hysteria isn't going to help anyone.' Ava dropped back against her chair, exhausted. A child born to a young unwed mother could destroy them if word got out. But she had to help Katie. Too many young women in her situation had been fished dead out of the Thames. There were few options for a penniless girl.

'You're going to have to have this baby,' she said. 'I can't agree to anything else since the alternative could kill you.'

'I don't want a baby!' Katie hunched over again.

'What about adoption?' Henry said from behind his paper.

Ava hesitated. The child of a working

girl would be more likely to join the dozens of fellow infants in the workhouse. And even if adoption could be arranged, Katie might bond with the child once it was born.

'I was considering fostering,' Ava said. 'Not in a baby farm, but with a decent family with an experienced, loving mother. We would have to pay, of course.'

'How much money?' Katie said. 'I don't earn that much.'

'I doubt you would be able to pay.' Ava sighed. 'The Orchid would have to take on the cost.'

'No, it can't,' Henry said. 'It's a business, not a charity.'

'What do you suggest then?'

He put down the paper. 'You can't pay the wages as it is. How do you seriously expect to pay a foster parent?'

'I'll not go to the workhouse. I'll throw myself in the Thames first,' Katie wailed.

'I don't recall ever mentioning the workhouse,' Henry said. He cleared his throat. 'I'll pay the fostering fees out of my own money, but if this happens again, Katie, you're on your own. Once is a mistake, but twice and you're foolish beyond saving.'

Katie sobbed louder.

'Thank you, Mr Scott-Leigh,' Ava said, her shoulders relaxing. 'We'll have to arrange a place for you to stay until the baby is born though, Katie. Do you have any family you can trust?'

Katie shook her head. 'Don't send me away. I'll keep hidden — stay in the kitchen with Cook.'

'You can't remain inside for five months.'

'Please! I've never lived anywhere else.'

Ava pressed her lips together. The young girl was white-faced and shaking. If she pushed her too far she might well follow through with her plan of throwing herself in the Thames. 'You can stay for now, if you wear loose clothing — but when the bump becomes too noticeable, we'll have to make other arrangements. Now go to your room Katie, and be glad that things haven't turned out worse for you.' Ava looked at the girl's white face and red eyes, then reached forwards to touch her shoulder. 'It'll be all right, don't worry. We're all here for you.'

'Thank you, Miss Miller.'

'Ava,' she said, but Katie had already run out of the room.

Slumping into her chair, Ava closed her eyes, head aching and limbs heavy as if she'd been up all night.

'I guess you'll be playing Belle for a bit longer yet,' Henry said.

'I'll train Daisy up. She's not quite as lively as Katie, but she'll do.'

'We can't have someone 'just doing'. The future of the theatre rests on this play being a success.'

'My whole life depends on this being a success. It's all right for you — you'll head back up north to live with your rich family in a mansion, while my cast and I search the streets in London for work. Don't accuse me of not understanding the importance of our situation.'

'I don't live in a mansion. I have my own home, a townhouse. I was staying with my family whilst I recovered from my injuries and found work, but I won't return there after leaving The Orchid.'

Ava stared at him. It was surprising, after the intensity of working together, how little she actually knew about him. 'Who do you live with?' she said.

'Myself, apart from a couple of maids, a cook and a valet. I certainly don't have a butler or a private lake.'

'Your family home is huge. My father visited it once. Why don't you stay there?'

'Because I prefer my own company. My family and I have never been close; I have little in common with them. For them, it is all about the business and money.'

'I assumed it was for you too?'

He smiled and folded up his paper. 'They don't believe I can make a success of The Orchid with a woman in charge. My father passed it over to me to deal with because he thought you were beyond rescue. My brief was to put in new management.'

Her mouth dried. 'Then why am I still here?'

'Because I thought you deserved a chance. It was clear when I first met you how much you love this place.'

'You felt sorry for me?'

'Not sorrow. Respect. I respected you for fighting for the theatre, even though it could have left you in a debtors' gaol.'

'And you also agreed to take on the cost of Katie's baby. You know what will happen if word of that gets out?'

'The child will be assumed to be mine. I am well aware of what will be presumed, but I don't care. Let people think what they will; it won't damage my reputation.'

'Because it's not unusual for a man to get an actress pregnant?'

'That's right; it's the sad way of the world.'

'I should be angry, but I can't be

cross with someone who has agreed to pay for a child he has no connection with.'

He looked at her. 'It pains me to see a child suffer. You assume that it doesn't bother me, but I have seen sights in war that would make the streets of London look a desirable place to live.'

'I feel I may have misjudged your character. You were so eager to get rid of Amelia, I thought you would do the same to Katie.'

'Amelia needs professional help. In her current state she is not long for this world. I don't know how much she is drinking, but I suspect it's more than most grown men could take.'

Ava glanced towards the door. She didn't like to talk about her girls, but if he understood Amelia's situation, he might be more inclined to help. It would be a relief to share the burden with someone — often her responsibilities were a heavy weight on her shoulders.

'Walter found Amelia on the street outside the Orchid. She'd been beaten and violated by a group of men. Later, we found she had been left with child.'

Henry drew in his breath sharply.

'She lost the child halfway through her term; the injuries she'd suffered were too extreme.' Ava folded her hands and looked at him. 'I know she's an alcoholic, but I'm not throwing her out. She has a lovely voice and, when sober, sings beautifully. But her days of sobriety are getting fewer. I have taken her to doctors and convents — everything I can — but I can't stop her drinking since she has no will to live. Amelia is likely not going to be around much longer, but until she passes on, she'll stay with me. She will be cared for because she has had precious little compassion until now.'

Henry nodded. 'You would be better running a home for waifs and strays than a theatre.'

'Are you implying that I'm a poor manageress?'

'I am stating the truth — that you are a kind woman.'

'If my father hadn't taken me in, I would have died on the streets. My mother never would have kept me close, as she cared nothing for me.'

'Well, he was your father.'

Ava hesitated. 'We hoped he was, but in truth, there is no proof. My mother was an actress with many admirers. I don't look like my father, but he took me in and raised me as his own, with love and care. It is my duty too, within my means, to follow his example. And while it might not make the most business sense, I know that I can wake up in the morning and hold my head high.'

'You must see, though, that if we make a success of this theatre, then you can help more people; we could set up a fund for the poor, apprenticeships for youngsters. But in order to help others, we must first help ourselves.'

'I think the two can go together. It is

not necessary to be hard-hearted to be a success.'

'I'm not talking about being cold. But the nature of a business is to make money, and at the moment you are making precious little. I admire your charitable concerns — you wouldn't be the woman you are without them — but there is also a case for making money, else you won't be able to support your inclinations.'

She glanced at him and his gaze, dark under the shadows from the fire, caught her own and heat rose to her skin. Why did she react like this to him? They had nothing common; they were from very different worlds. Then Henry strode over towards her and reached down to take her hands.

Ava pulled away.

'You feel the same as I do,' he said, his voice soft.

'I feel nothing.' She tried to stand up, but he blocked her way.

'I know it's wrong. There can't be anything between us — every part of me tells me that — but I can't stop thinking about you.'

Breathing deep, she looked at him. 'If it's wrong, then you should leave me alone. What good could come of it?'

'So you do feel something?'

She hesitated and moistened her lips. He was right — she was desperate to reach out her arms and hold him, feel the hard muscles she watched flexing beneath his shirt, kiss the lips that had touched hers while they'd skated. He made her feel safe and desired. If this was love, then it was like nothing she'd ever felt before. This was more than she could deal with. To be so aware of him standing in front to her; to know that if she held out her arms, he would hold her tight, kiss her.

'Please, leave me alone,' she said. 'No good could ever come of it. As you pointed out, we are from different worlds, and I would never be a mistress.'

'I would wed you. I want to see you every morning at my breakfast table; I want to sleep knowing you lie beside me. But I would also be disowned by my family. And if I am thrown out from my family, you would lose The Orchid. And I know how you love it so.'

'It is the theatre that holds you back?'

'It is you that holds me back. I would rather sleep alone than know that I had hurt you, brought trouble to that door that has dealt with so much already. You have far greater responsibilities than I, and duties you feel keenly. We could be together, but you would have to give up the theatre and your friends because I wouldn't have the money to support you all.'

'And Katie's baby?'

He swallowed. 'It would be difficult on the stipend I receive from the army. I don't intend to remain working for my family, though — my father can be a vindictive man. I want to strike out alone and set up my own businesses, run the way I want to run them. It will take time, though; at least five years, I suspect. Would you be willing to wait for me?'

'Henry, this is too much. This is the first time you have mentioned your feelings for me, and now you ask me to put my life on hold for five years so you can make enough money for us to wed. I haven't even said that I wish for us to marry; you haven't even asked me.'

'I can't ask you yet, not until I have earned enough to support a wife. I couldn't ask you to marry a man with no means.'

'I would marry a man with no money at all if I loved him.'

'Which I couldn't allow you to do. Poverty isn't romantic, as you know well — it's a killer with starvation, disease. All those things you would risk for me? And what of your staff? Katie and her baby? Amelia? Is that what you'd wish for them too? No, Ava, I know you too well already. You would be miserable if you believed you'd let them down. If I take you on, I accept your responsibilities too.'

'So I am a burden? No, Henry, I

won't wait for you. I know that when you leave here, returning to the ballrooms of your birth, you will quickly forget the actress who caught your eye. You don't approve of me or my lifestyle and I won't become a china statue in a drawing room for you. I am a working girl and that is how I will remain.'

'You don't think I know my own mind?'

'I believe you are recently injured and separated from your friends, so you think yourself in love with me, but you are not. How could you be when you have made it so clear how different we are?'

'I know what I feel. I lie in bed at night picturing your face; I listen to you when you are talking to others so that I can hear the sound of your voice. Don't try to convince me it is nothing. And I think you feel the same. You won't look me in the eye anymore or walk beside me. When we went skating, you didn't pull away when I kissed you.'

'I was surprised.'

Henry stepped forward to stand in front of her, his body against hers. Ava tried to move back, but the hard wood of the settle dug into her knees. Leaning down, he pressed his lips to hers, his mouth warm and inviting, his stubble against her cheeks. She leaned forward, deeper into his embrace, her body betraying her true feelings. Of course she loved him; she had since the day she had walked into the parlour and seen him sitting there, with his scarred face and intelligent, kind eyes. Henry was the perfect man for her, supportive and thoughtful, yet a man of action. She wanted him and The Orchid needed him, but soon he would leave. He wasn't meant for the uncertain and bawdy life of the theatre. And certainly, she couldn't be the reason he was cast out by his family. Without relatives of her own, she knew too well how much it hurt to be alone in the world, and the guilt would destroy her.

No, she couldn't have Henry, so this

infatuation must end. She wanted him so much though. Pulling away from him, she looked down.

'This can't be,' she said. 'And I am sorry for it, because I do feel the same way. But our circumstances are such that we could never be happy together.'

'Then we must change those circumstances.'

'And how? By you being thrown out by your family, and me losing The Orchid and my friends? They depend on me; I can't desert them. If we could keep the theatre, then we could stay here together; but without that, I don't see how we could ever be happy.'

'So you would choose the theatre over me?'

'I would have to choose the people I have grown up with, whom I care for, because I can't desert them. And if you think I would be willing to do so, even for love, then you don't know me at all.'

'I never thought that. It's what I have been telling you is the problem. I did think you might wait for me though, but since you show so little inclination to find a solution I can only imagine that I must have mistaken your regard.' Twisting around his heel, Henry strode towards the door. 'Good night, madam. I will not bother you further.'

Ava watched him go, then flung herself onto the settle. If she abandoned her actors, the men might manage to find other jobs, but Katie and Amelia certainly would not — and what of Daisy, shy little Daisy? She'd be destroyed if she lost the only family she knew. They were a mixed group, but the one thing they all had in common was that at The Orchid they had found an acceptance that the rest of society had denied them. They were a family, albeit an unusual one, and she couldn't desert them.

Rising to her feet, Ava wrapped her arms around her shivering body and blinked back tears, as Henry's feet trod a heavy step up the stairs. She had lost him. In despair, she picked up the newspaper and instinctively turned to the entertainment section, casting her eyes down the theatre reviews until she spotted The Orchid. Hopefully, they'd get some good news here at least; the audience had been enthusiastic. The review started well with praise for the script and Walter, and she smiled — until she read the next part, which described her own entrance onto the stage.

'Ava Miller stumbled with her words, seemed uncertain and often looked to be standing in the wrong place. She brought down this adaptation of an otherwise excellent play. She is too old to play the part of a young girl and twice had to be rescued by other cast members. For a woman who also manages the theatre, serious questions should be asked by the owners over whether she is up to the task.'

Mouth dropping open, she dropped the paper onto the settle. She'd let everyone down by not learning those damn lines. What if the rest of the Scott-Leigh family saw that? What would they think of her abilities?

There were footsteps outside the door and she looked up to see Henry standing there, looking at her.

'I came back to collect that, as I didn't want you to see it,' he said. 'Daisy read it out this morning to me.'

'I needed to see it since I'm the manageress.' She glanced down at the paper. 'At the moment, anyway.' Ava closed her eyes. It had been a disaster, and all due to her. She should have employed a proper understudy. 'I'm sorry,' she said.

'Don't be sorry. It's not your fault.'

'I think we both know that it is.' She looked at the floor, not daring to catch his gaze. Goodness, she was tired. Could she run this theatre alone? There was so much work to do, and little money to pay for help. She had creditors knocking at the door and the constant pressure from the Scott-Leigh family to make a profit. And on top of all that, she had to work beside a man she loved but couldn't have.

Putting her hands over her face, she dropped her head down, shoulders shaking as she sobbed. It had all been too much, and to have let everyone down when they had worked so hard to make this play a success . . . What must Henry think of her? She'd shown herself up. Her father never would have made such an error.

A warm hand touched her shoulder and she shook her head. 'Leave me alone, please,' she said.

'It's late. Come to bed.'

She thought of another night of staring at the cracks in the ceiling, a pain clenching her stomach, and shook her head. 'I wouldn't sleep. I'll go to the kitchen and make a hot drink. My throat hurts.'

'From being on stage?'

She nodded, though it was tension that gripped her throat.

His hand squeezed. 'Go and tuck yourself up in bed. I'll make you a hot chocolate drink and bring it up to you. It's cold, and sitting here freezing isn't going to make you feel any better.'

She nodded, straightening her shoulders. It was nice to have someone take control for a short time. Her papa would have said something similar; how she missed his calm presence.

'Can you do that?' she said.

His lip quirked. 'Yes, Ava, I can make a hot chocolate. Now off you go and get into bed. I'll be in soon, so pull your covers up high.'

'I doubt you would be shocked if I didn't. For someone who has such high morals, I suspect you have more of a past then you are letting on.'

He smiled and holding her arm, pulled her to her feet.

Climbing the stairs, she wrapped her shawl around her shoulders, wishing it was his arms around her. Tonight she didn't want to be alone in her bed. She could understand why Katie took the risk she did. The temptation to have someone hold you close, stroke your hair and say they loved you was overwhelming at times. But she could never take the risk.

Stepping into her bedroom, she glanced at the small fire, made with fresh coal so recently lit. Henry must have done it, knowing she was upset and in need of comfort tonight. Taking a candle from the table, she lit it from the flames and set it into its holder. The tiny light flared, casting shadows over the walls, highlighting the clouds of white mist as she exhaled her breath. Crossing to the washing stand, she poured a small amount of tepid water from the jug into the basin and hastily washed before pulling off her gown, petticoats and stays. Clad in woollen stockings and bloomers, she scrambled into a chilly cotton nightdress.

There were footsteps outside her room and she hastily pulled back the covers to climb into bed, yanking the covers high so only her face showed. Too late, she remembered her nightcap. Her hair lay strewn over the pillow, gleaming in the firelight in a way only a husband should see. She couldn't fetch it now — the door was pushing open. Better that Henry see her hair down than the shape of her body in her nightgown. In truth, they'd both be shamed if anyone knew he had visited her room at all, even for the innocent task of delivering a hot drink. Clarence would be especially shocked, since he'd become very possessive lately.

A dark shadow cast across the floor as Henry strode towards her bed, the scent of rich, sweet chocolate filling the room. 'Here,' he said, placing the cup on the bedside table. 'Are you warm enough?'

She nodded, her teeth chattering. 'Did you light the fire for me?'

'I felt guilty for upsetting you. It was wrong of me to expect you to choose. Of course you would select your friends here. They need you.'

'They can't do without me.'

'I'm not sure I can.'

'Henry, please.'

'It frustrates me that something which should be so simple, falling in

147

love, can end up so complicated.'

'I doubt it is ever simple.' She reached over to take the mug, wrapping her shaking fingers around the hot china.

He sat down on the edge of the bed and she jumped back against her pillows, spilling some of her drink.

'Henry, this is not appropriate.'

'I don't think you really care about that. You're a woman of the world, not a blushing girl on her first trip out.'

'So you believe I don't have a reputation to maintain?'

'I don't think anyone is out on the landing listening and even if they are, your actors will always protect you.'

Ava sipped her drink, a warmth spreading out across her stomach. Settling back against the pillow, she closed her eyes. Henry shouldn't be here, she should ask him to leave, but it was so comforting having him sit beside her. Opening her eyes, she stared at him and he gazed back, eyes narrowed, his expression mirroring her own thoughts.

Henry cleared his throat. 'I should go,'

His warm hand touched her own and she froze, then relaxed as he squeezed gently, then left the room. Raising herself on her elbows, she picked up the snuffer and put out the candle.

★ ★ ★

Waking in the morning, she smiled at the memory of his touch. Henry was a man of honour; he'd never take advantage of her. Sitting up, she hugged her knees in her nightgown, breath frosting in the morning air. Sliding out of bed, she glanced at the charred sticks in the fireplace, then pulling on a dressing gown and thrusting her feet into slippers, she went out onto the landing and down the stairs.

Opening the kitchen door, she jumped. Clarence sat on one of the chairs, his head on the table cushioned by an arm and an empty glass standing beside him. Breathing in the sharp smell of spirits, she frowned. What on earth was he doing? Clarence never usually drank, and certainly not enough to pass out at the kitchen table. Soon Cook would come down and wake him up by clattering her fire irons and kettle.

Creeping over to the range, she picked up a bucket and quietly, piece by piece, transferred a few chunks of coal from the main scuttle. There, that should be enough. She'd leave off making tea for now, but would freshen her mouth with a drink of cold water. Taking a cup, she filled it from the pump, keeping a careful eye on the sleeping form. Had he moved? She didn't want him to wake, which was strange because he'd been her best friend until Henry had arrived. Had Clarence noticed her withdrawal? She must make more time for him. It wasn't fair to desert him because another man had arrived to take her interest.

He moved on the table and she leapt back, grabbing the handle of the coal bucket. Creeping towards the door, she stepped through into the hall and glanced back over her shoulder. Clarence was awake, staring after her with eyes red-rimmed and mouth set and angry. He looked like the cross little boy she remembered from their childhood.

'Just getting some coal,' she said.

'I saw you,' he said.

'Saw me?' She swallowed, nausea rising from her throat. He could only mean with Henry. Had he spotted Henry going into her room? Why would Clarence be near her chamber though? He slept in the men's quarters, leading from the other landing.

'Saw you.' He dropped his head back onto the table. Ava closed the door and stood with her back to it, coal bucket slipping in her sweating, shaking hands. Why would it matter that Clarence had seen them? He was hardly going to judge, was he? He'd had plenty of women himself, generally young actresses wanting a part — she suspected he took advantage of them, but it wasn't her business. If the girls were that way inclined, there was nothing she could do for them. He never touched her girls, she was sure of that.

Walking into the parlour, she jumped again. Henry was sitting on the settle, dressed and with wet hair. He reached out a hand towards her scuttle.

'I was going to fetch that,' he said. 'It's not a job for you.'

She laughed. 'Do you have any idea how many coal scuttles I carry around this place? Of course it's a woman's job, as many a parlour maid could testify to.'

'I meant it wasn't a job I expected you to be doing as a manageress.'

'I think you have a lot to learn still about The Orchid.' Kneeling by the fire, she took a handful of small twigs and paper from the box beside the grate and nestled them in the ashes. Taking a box of matches from the mantle, she struck one, wrinkling her nose at the smell of sulphur, before holding it to the paper. As it took light, she piled the coals around.

'See,' she said, smiling over her shoulder. 'My talents are many. We work together here; there are no servants except Cook, and she orders us around more than we instruct her. It's the way the theatre has always been run.'

Henry walked over, crouching beside her on the rug and taking her hand.

'I'm covered in smuts,' she said.

'I don't care.' He turned her wrist and planted a kiss on her clean, soft underarm, tracing his lips up towards her elbow. She shivered and rested against him, enjoying the warmth of his body through her thin night clothing.

'I like the way you run things here,' he said. 'I never fitted in with my father's house. He's a self-made millionaire and likes to ensure that everyone knows it, so the downstairs rooms are lavish and at dinner parties he serves the best champagne. Upstairs, the family bedrooms are stark and cold. After all, none of our guests go into those, so why waste the money? It is all for show and no part of it has ever felt like a home.'

'Do you like your father?'

He hesitated. 'We are civil, but not close. I am not the son he wanted, but luckily since I have two brothers, I could go my own way. At least until I was injured and had to return to the family firm.'

'How could you not be what he wanted?' She frowned. Henry was a decorated soldier, an honourable and intelligent man. Who wouldn't want him as a member of their family?

'He is not military-minded. I went into the army because he didn't consider me to be any use in the business. For my family, even my mother and sister, it is all about making money. The talk over the table in the evening is about profits and losses. Nothing else matters to them except expanding their already considerable dynasty.'

She nodded, noting he hadn't included

himself as part of that dynasty. Henry didn't feel a part of it at all.

'You wanted to make a success of The Orchid to prove to your family that you could be a businessman?'

'At first. I have a desire to do my best in any situation.' He smiled. 'Do I sound like my family now?'

'I have met your brothers and you are nothing like them, either in looks or temperament.'

'Sadly, though, I cannot deny they are my family.' Standing, he reached down and rested his hands on her shoulders. 'I must return to my room before people start to question us.'

'I suspect Clarence already knows.'

Henry froze. 'It might not be a good idea to tell him too much. He isn't happy about me being here. He could cause problems when I have left.'

'There is nothing wrong with Clarence, only that I have neglected him. Until you arrived, he was the one I turned to. It has been so busy recently, but I must make sure I spend more time with him. He's worked hard for this theatre; he was born here.'

'Does he have family?'

'Not living. His mother was an unwed actress who starred in one of our productions, but we didn't realise until later that she was pregnant. Unlike Katie, her dress was very loose and her belly small. She went into labour, but didn't survive. The doctor said she was poorly nourished and suffering from consumption. My father took Clarence on.'

'So he is like a brother to you?'

'Yes.'

'Then it is surprising you were engaged.'

She stopped and stared at the flickering flames of the fire. She couldn't admit she lied, not to this honest man.

'It was short-lived, ill-advised and hastily rushed into.' That at least was true. 'There were no true feelings there.'

'I suspect there are on his side, more

then you realise. Be careful of him, Ava. There is something about him that worries me.'

'Don't be ridiculous! I know him far better than you do. Don't become jealous. You can't offer me a future and there will never be anything more between us than stolen kisses.'

'I'm just warning you; don't heed if you don't wish to.' He stepped back. 'I'll see you at breakfast, madam.' Inclining his head towards her, he strode out of the room.

* * *

Ava pulled out her office chair and sat down, sinking her head into her hands. What a mess! One moment she and Henry were close; the next, arguing about Clarence. The door opened and Daisy strode in with the morning post. More bills — just what she needed to cheer herself up!

'Are you all right, Miss Miller?' Daisy said, putting the letters on the desk.

'You look a bit peaky.'

She certainly wasn't going to tell the girl the truth: that she had fallen in love with Henry. 'I'm fine,' she said. 'A touch of a cold, maybe.'

'Not the same type Katie has?'

'Daisy!'

The girl grinned. 'Sorry, miss, couldn't resist. She's up in her bed hiding under the covers. Amelia's just taken her some porridge up.'

'That was nice of her.'

Daisy shuffled her feet, looking down. 'Are you going to send Katie away?'

'She'll have to go away to have the baby, but she can come back afterwards.'

'And what about the child?'

'It will be fostered for now. When she gets married, if her husband agrees, she can take the little one back.'

'So unless she finds a man, she's going to lose her baby?'

Ava sighed. 'What else would you have me do? She can't live here, even in a theatre, with a bastard child. We'd all be ruined. I'm willing to support Katie, but I can't work miracles. She's lucky; most places would have thrown her out by now.'

'It's a shame though.'

'She'll be able to see the baby regularly.' Ava looked at Daisy. 'Is she upset? It that why you're asking these questions?'

'She hasn't said anything, other than she doesn't want a child and that Mr Scott-Leigh is going to be looking after it. But she looks miserable.'

'Mr Scott-Leigh isn't caring for the child — be careful about saying that, Daisy. People will get the wrong idea. He has offered out of charitable kind-ness to pay for a foster parent. That's as far as his connection with it goes.'

'Oh, I wasn't saying that he was anything to do with the baby. I know whose it is.'

'We're all going to have to keep it quiet and not talk to anyone, else Katie will have to leave. She can only stay here if we keep it secret.'

'I can do her shopping for her.'

'That would be very kind of you. And Daisy,' she said, as the girl turned to go, 'thank you for your understanding. It's a bad situation Katie's got herself into, but not that uncommon either. Just don't do the same, please. I can't cope with two of you.'

Daisy shook her head, mouth open. 'Never, miss. Not me, nor Amelia again. She says she'd cut the balls off any man who came near her.'

Ava choked back a laugh — it was good to see that Amelia still had some sense of self-preservation. 'I wouldn't recommend quite such a violent reaction. Stepping away is sufficient usually. If he persists, then scream loudly and kick him in the shins.'

'All right, miss.' Daisy grinned and ran out the door.

Ava picked up the post and slit the first envelope. It had the printed crest of the Scott-Leigh family along the top. Frowning, she turned the missive over to check the name. It was definitely for her. How strange. With Henry in the house she would have expected correspondence from his father to be addressed to him. It was probably on too small a topic to be worth bothering him with.

Folding the single sheet of paper, she began to read.

Miss Miller

I am most displeased by the reviews of our current play, which Henry assured me would be the making of the theatre. It appears that even with his help, you are incapable of running The Orchid. Therefore I have instructed my lawyers to look into the selling of the theatre. Pass this information onto my son and tell him has to return home tomorrow.

Mr. Scott-Leigh.

Ava dropped over her desk, stomach clenching. How could he do this to them? To not even give them a chance of making the play work! It had been her responsibility to ensure every part had a correctly trained understudy and she'd failed. Caught up in the renovations of the theatre, she'd been distracted from the most important part of putting on the play: the performance itself. Her strongest abilities weren't in mending buildings or creating money. She excelled at putting on plays, at casting and training the actors. But this time she'd failed — too caught up with money worries and thinking about Henry. Now they'd all lost their home. What would they do? Katie was pregnant, Amelia a drunk. How could she support them all?

The door pushed open again and she looked up as Henry strode in through the door, jaw set and eyes narrowed.

'We need to talk,' he said.

Dropping the poisonous little letter onto her desk, she pushed it towards him. 'A letter from your father.'

'He wouldn't write to me.'

'It's addressed to me, but concerns

you. Read it, please. It's important.'

He hesitated and reached to take the paper, folding it in half.

'Read it now, Henry!'

'I'll take it to my lawyer, as I do all letters of business.'

'It's not a legal note.'

Snatching it back, she opened it, then went still. Henry had never read anything in her presence; he avoided the scripts and got Daisy to read the paper to him after breakfast. She'd assumed he was teaching the girl to improve her English, but maybe it wasn't Daisy with the problem.

'Why does your father doubt your abilities to run a business?' she said.

'I'm a military man.'

She looked up at him, standing tall and proud in front of her, his eyes gazing into hers and chin lifted in a challenging expression. Ava swallowed.

'You can't read, can you, Henry?' she said.

He stared down at her, jaw clenched. 'I wondered how long it would take you to notice. Longer than I expected, actually. Yes, you're right, I can't read. Your little Daisy is better with her letters than I am.'

'I taught her.' Ava moistened her lips. 'Did you not attend school?'

'I went to the top schools in England, had private tutors and goodness knows what kind of money poured into my schooling. It made no difference. I can't fathom letters. Numbers I can do, but letters jump around, turn backwards. I can't fit them together. I can read after a fashion, but it takes me a long time to translate a letter. In the army, my batman did it for me.'

'So this is why you have differences with your father and brothers?'

'Yes; they believe I am stupid.' He raised his head. 'But I'm not, I just can't read. No one has ever been able to understand why — the masters used force and the cane to persuade me, but it made no difference. My brain just doesn't work that way.'

Ava looked at him. Henry was clearly

a highly intelligent man. She'd heard of a couple of actors who learnt their part in a play by having the script read to them, so maybe it wasn't that unusual. Henry stepped around the desk and reached down to take her hand.

'This is why I can't just ask you to join me, even though I have fallen in love with you. I can't support you easily. I only have this job due to my family. If I wed without their agreement, I would be penniless.'

'I can pay my own way. I am considered an actress of some talent. Is all this drama just an excuse? We're hardly Romeo and Juliet, torn apart by circumstances beyond our control. If we wanted to be together, then nothing should part us, not family or money.'

'But it does matter though, doesn't it? Are you telling me that you'd walk out of The Orchid tonight, leaving everyone, in order to marry me?'

She hesitated. Henry was right, she couldn't do it. Her sense of duty wouldn't allow her to. However much she wanted him, it was impossible to go against her nature and desert those who relied on her.

'So where do we go from here?' she said.

Henry brought his fist down on her desk with a bang, making her jump. 'I don't know,' he said. 'I wish I could see a way around it, but there isn't one. My family would never accept you, and by defying them, we would lose the theatre.'

'Could we raise funds and buy it ourselves?'

'Not unless you have a ready source of income you haven't mentioned to me.'

Her gaze fell on the sheet of paper from his father. 'I am going to lose The Orchid anyway,' she said. 'Your father has ordered you to go home immediately and for the theatre to be shut. I am no longer the manageress.'

'He said that?' Henry's eyes narrowed.

She almost held the paper out, then

remembered and placed it back on the table. 'I'll read it out; it is short and to the point.' She did so, gratified that his fists clenched.

'It is also rude,' he said.

'I am his employee, an unwanted worker. He has no reason to be polite.'

'I will dictate a letter back immediately, telling him that the theatre has a chance and that it needs more time.'

'You're not going to return home?'

'No. I'm not going to respond to a summons like that.' Henry's jaw tightened. 'My father is a difficult man, cold and uncaring. The only way to deal with him is to stand your ground. Once he thinks he can push you around, you'll be destroyed by his malicious game-playing. So we're going to put this play on until the end of its run, regardless of what he wants. The only way he'll get this place shut down is to come down here himself and physically do it. I'm certainly not going to. There's so much potential here.'

'Do you think so?'

'Of course; with work and the right shows, this place could make lots of money.'

'Maybe I'm the wrong person to manage it?'

He glanced at her and nausea rose from her stomach when he didn't contradict her. Why would he? It was obvious to anyone that she was failing the place as its manager. Her father had managed it successfully for years, but in less than six months she'd driven it almost into bankruptcy.

'Let's carry on with the run of the play. We're due a couple more critics later in the week. If we put on a better show, we'll get good reviews. For a first night, they weren't that bad.'

'They weren't that good either, and the theatre industry is unforgiving. People have paid good money to see the play and they expect the best.'

'Then that's what we'll give them.' He glanced at her. 'You look exhausted; when did you last do anything other than work?'

She almost said when they went ice-skating, but that was something she doubted he wanted reminding of. 'A while, I think,' she said.

'I'm due to go out to dinner tonight at a private house. Come with me as my dinner guest?'

She raised her eyebrows. 'That would certainly set the gossips wondering. I can imagine the expression on your hostess's face when she realises you have brought an unwed actress to dinner.'

'I wasn't going to mention that part.' He grinned, his face looking younger and carefree. 'I'll have to invite a chaperone too.'

'A lady with a steely eye and sharp tongue?'

'No, a friendly woman who offers to accompany young ladies out, in return for their company. It is Mrs Richards, the parent of our playwright.'

'At least I need not fear a comely young widow with a gleam in her eye.'

'You need fear none. I have never

met anyone like you in any drawing room.'

'I know — that's what I'm afraid of. I won't fit in, Henry. I'm not a society lady.'

'You'll be fine. Just don't swear or drink too much port.'

'Since when have you known me do either?'

'I'm teasing, Ava. You behave impeccably, even if you can yell like a market trader when you want to. As an actress I'm sure you'll be able to charm them all, and in the meantime, you'll be able to have a delicious dinner and a seat by a warm fire.'

'It's tempting, if you think it won't damage your reputation?'

'I'm a single, wealthy gentleman; it takes a lot to ruin my reputation, especially amongst the mothers of young girls. Do you have a suitable dress?'

'I have a theatre of frocks to choose from. I could go as Cleopatra, or Aladdin — even a pantomime horse.'

'I think the horse would be the best choice — then I could sit beside you without anyone noticing you're a woman.' He smiled. 'But I may not have such a good view of your shoulders.'

She looked down at the shawl she'd wrapped tightly around her bodice. 'I'd probably be wearing less than I do in this damned freezing office each day. The new fires help, but the dampness has sunk into the very walls.'

''Damned' is the word you're not supposed to say.' Reaching forward, he laid his hand on hers and leaned down. 'I wonder what our hostess would think if she'd seen us in your room last night,' he whispered mischievously.

Heat rose to Ava's cheeks. Was he implying that she had done something wrong? Raising her head, she caught his eye and sighed in relief as his lips curled up in a smile. Stepping closer, he reached down, his arm sliding over her wrap and encircling her neck, his hand moving to raise her jaw.

'So beautiful,' he said.

Bending, he kissed her gently, then harder, his mouth and tongue tingling her senses as they lovingly explored her own. Moving down, he traced his lips across her jaw and when she raised her neck, down her throat in light butterfly kisses, each followed by a brief pause as if he stopped to savour her skin. Ava reached her arms up and looped them around his neck, her body twisting in her chair. His stubble brushed her cheeks, his mouth hot as he loosened her shawl and pushed it back to stroke her collarbone.

The door slammed open and Ava threw herself straight, pulling away. Clarence stood in the doorway, eyes darkening with a fury she'd never seen before. Was he trying to protect her? But she needed no protection; with Henry she was as safe as with her own father.

'I knew you were taking advantage of her,' Clarence shouted. 'Because she hasn't got any family to look after her, you think she's fair game. Well, I'm not going to let you hurt her. Go and find another mistress.'

'You've got it wrong,' Ava said. 'He's not making me do anything I don't want to do.'

'You can't desire this man. Look at him. Have you seen his scars?'

'That's enough!' Henry said. 'What we do is none of your business. You're no longer engaged to Miss Miller. She's a free woman who can make her own decisions.'

'But she can't, can she? Because she's frightened you'll take her home off her and send her away from the people who know and love her. She's going along with you to save herself from destitution.'

'That isn't true,' Ava said. 'I wouldn't sell myself for anything.'

'What else do you think you are doing? If you believe he's going to marry you, you're sorely mistaken. Men of his class don't wed poor actresses! There's only one reason he's paying attention to you, and that's to get into your bed — and from what I saw the other night, that's something he's succeeding with.' Clarence stared at Ava with contempt. 'It didn't take long, did it? You're a hussy, Ava Miller! And you dare criticise Katie for the same thing. At least she thought she was getting married.'

'How dare you!' she said, staring at him wide-eyed in shock. 'You forget yourself. I've done nothing wrong. We only talked. It may not have been within the strictest bounds of propriety, I grant you, but we didn't do what you are insinuating.'

'Get out, Clarence, before I turn you out of this theatre!' Henry said, stepping in front of Ava. 'The only reason you are still here is because I can accept that you are grieved about the end of your own engagement, but if you continue to speak to Miss Miller in this way, I'll turn you out without a reference.'

'I'm saying nothing that isn't the truth. She's a slut.'

Henry's fist shot out, smashing Clarence on the side of his head with a thud, knocking him across the room.

'No,' Ava said, shoving back her chair and racing around her desk.

'Keep back,' Henry pulled her behind him.

'No, I will not. Clarence is my friend. I know he's upset now, but you don't understand how worried he is about The Orchid. He's my assistant manager and you have no right to hit him.'

'But he has a right to insult you?'

'I know you're a soldier, but this is not a battlefield and Clarence isn't your enemy.'

'I give up.' Henry spaced his hands out. 'Go to him if you want, but I warn you that his intentions towards you aren't honourable.'

'And yours are?' Clarence said, pulling himself into a sitting position, a hand to his mouth.

'Enough, both of you!' Ava said, pulling a handkerchief from her pocket. Dropping it beside Clarence, she strode out of the room, leaving them behind her. A few yards down the corridor, she turned as the sound of footsteps echoed behind her. It was Clarence, her handkerchief clutched to his face, stained red.

'I'm sorry, Ava,' he said. 'But that man is insufferable. How much longer do we have to put up with him lording over us?'

'I think he's been kind, actually, and has listened to us all. You must try to accept him; we need his help. And you certainly should not have said those things about me. I have never been any man's mistress.'

'I know, and I'm sorry; I was angry.' He stopped and looked down at her, his familiar blue eyes sad, his mouth bruised beneath.

'Please, just try to get along with him. He won't be here that long, and if his father has his way, we'll be shut down by the end of the week anyway. Compared to being homeless, your petty squabble doesn't really matter very much. What do you think is going to happen to us all? To Katie, to Amelia? Unless I find a way to save them, it'll be the workhouse for both of them and we both know what goes on in those places.'

Blinking, she swallowed as a hard lump gathered in her throat. What on earth would they all do? They were a family here, but now they'd be separated; thrown out into the cold, rough streets of London. Wiping her eyes, she remembered the evenings they'd spent together in the parlour after a performance — the men with ale, the girls with hot toddies, flames flickering in the fire, and her father seated beside her. It had been so much easier then. This was what Henry didn't have — the shared memories she had of growing up alongside Clarence, learning their lessons together; of Daisy arriving as a young girl; Amelia being carried from the street, broken and bloodied. He didn't understand what bound them together.

Clarence nodded and put his hand on her arm. 'I'll stay away from him, but you need to be careful. He's out of your class.'

'I'm hardly a drudge.'

'You'd never be accepted by society and neither would he. You'd be separating him from his family and friends and it would be wrong of you to do that.'

Ava nodded. She hadn't thought of that before. Clarence was right, they would never be accepted by either side; even her fellow actors would treat her differently if she married a wealthy man. And she would never be able to work again. Not only would she have to give up The Orchid, but she would have to give up her acting, which she loved. So many sacrifices. Too many for a man she had only known a few weeks.

But she had never felt this way before about anyone. It hadn't been long, but what she felt for Henry was more than mere lust. It was his kindness and intelligence she loved — the care he took of her.

'It doesn't matter,' she said. 'You're right, we couldn't be together. He said the same thing.'

'You're the type of compassionate person at risk of losing your head over an unsuitable romance. I doubt you love him at all. He's probably just replacing your father; a steady army man is the sort of person you feel in need of now.' Clarence squeezed her arm, the grip over-tight. 'You're not alone though, Ava, even if it feels like you have the weight of all our problems on your shoulders. Let me help you, like I used to before he came along.'

Ava stepped away from him, but he retained his grasp.

'None of this is relevant at the moment,' she said. 'We've already lost the theatre, as Henry's father is insisting it is closed down and put up for sale. There is nothing else we can do.'

'Well, he'll have to travel down and

do it personally, because none of us will help him. Unless his son does.'

'Henry has said he won't.'

'I wouldn't fully trust him on that. Why should he be loyal to us? This money is from his family; without them he is penniless. Don't ever forget the power of cash.'

'True.' She nodded and moved back further to release her arm — he smelt of wine and it repulsed her in a way it never did with Amelia.

'Go and get cleaned up,' she said. 'I need to learn my script for tomorrow night so I'm word-perfect. Luckily there is no performance tonight.'

★ ★ ★

In the dressing room Ava hung two dresses on hooks on the wall and stepped back to examine them, narrowing her eyes under the flicking light of the candle. Which gown would be best for Henry's dinner party tonight? To her surprise, he had stopped her in the corridor to tell her they would leave at eight. She had assumed after the debacle with Clarence that the trip out had been forgotten. However it appeared Henry was determined to show her off to society. Was he really that desperate for a companion, or did he want to spend time with her, even though they couldn't have a future?

Looking critically at the dresses, she frowned. One was smooth satin the colour of a green apple, its bustle decorated with tiny seed pearls and light pink miniature bows along the demure neckline. The other was midnight-blue with lace trims across the long, close-fitting sleeves and a daring scoop top, lined with a velvet trim. It was the older, more sophisticated dress, but was it too much for a dinner party? She didn't want to give the wrong impression before her fellow diners even discovered her occupation.

The door opened behind her and she turned. Amelia leant against her door frame, her face thin and shallow under the dim shadows.

'Going out, miss?' she said.

'I am, to my surprise. A dinner party, of all things. I never expected to get invited to one of those.'

'I don't see why not. You're more beautiful than any of those posh ladies we get in here. And better read too.'

'Sadly it is all due to birth, and I was born the illegitimate daughter of a theatre manager. I'm not in a position to mingle with gentry. Which dress do you like?'

'The dark blue. The men in the audience can't take their eyes off you when you're on stage in that one.'

'But I will be on a different stage tonight, judged for more than my ability to deliver a perfect line. Do you think it will be fashionable enough? I wouldn't want to make the terrible mistake of having long sleeves when they should be short.'

'I reckon if you look beautiful, it won't matter what length your sleeves are. You can always tell them you've just come from abroad. Put on a French accent.'

Ava laughed and reached forward to touch Amelia's pinched face. 'Oh, my darling, I wish you could be going out dressed up and wearing fur.'

Amelia smiled. 'I don't need furs or dresses. I never wanted anything like that.'

Ava hugged the girl close, wincing as her sharp ribs dug into her chest. Amelia didn't have long left. She blinked away tears — such a wasted life, abused by most until she found sanctuary in The Orchid. But even within these four walls, she couldn't escape her past and, haunted by nightmares, sunk by depression, the drink was both her escape and her murderer. What would happen to her if they were forced to close?

Amelia stepped back, her hands trailing down Ava's back as if reluctant to let go. 'You'd better get ready,' she said. 'Wouldn't do to be late for Mr Henry.'

'What do you think of him?' Ava said, taking the midnight-blue dress down from the wall.

'I like him. He doesn't fuss, but if he meets me on the stairs he always takes my arm to help me up. First time I've been touched by a gentleman like that. Usually they weren't interested in my arm. You could do worse, miss!' She grinned, her face lighting up.

Leaning down to kiss the girl's cold cheek, Ava took off her shawl and wrapped it around Amelia's shoulders. 'You get up to bed and stay warm. Ask Cook to make you up a fire, on my orders.'

'Thanks, miss.'

Folding the dress over her arm, Ava hurried up the stairs to her room. Life truly was short when you were unlikely to reach your nineteenth birthday. Worrying about the theatre and Henry kept her awake at night, but really she ought to be thankful that she did at least have her health and a sound mind.

Henry stood at the bottom of the

stairs, wearing dark trousers and a dress shirt that gleamed in the dim hallway. He leant over the mirror, adjusting his cravat, and she looked away, guilty that he didn't have a looking-glass in his own room. Born into luxury, he had never complained about either of the rooms she'd given him — even the first, which she would think twice about putting a pet dog in.

Hesitating when he glanced at her, she held up the dress. 'Suitable?'

'Very. You'll look lovely. The carriage is due in half an hour.' He looked at her print dress and plaited hair.

'Don't worry, I'm used to changing fast. I'll be down in plenty of time.' Putting her head around the parlour door, she called, 'Daisy! Could you come up and help me dress?'

'Course,' Daisy said, stepping out of the room.

'I won't be long,' Ava said to Henry, her legs trembling as she turned to the stairs. Was it the effect of seeing him, or her nerves about tonight? While she'd played many a fine lady, she'd never been in a drawing room full of real ones.

Upstairs, Daisy unbuttoned Ava's dress and petticoats, slipping them off her arms.

'I'll need a bustle out of the cupboard,' Ava said. 'My current corset will do though.'

'I can tighten it,' Daisy said, taking the bustle out.

'No, thanks — I don't fancy passing out in the soup. I'm used to wearing working dresses.' Clad in stockings and corset, Ava turned around so Daisy could fasten the tapes of the bustle on and straighten it at the back.

'How's Katie?' she said. 'I haven't seen her all day.'

'Hiding in her bedroom, head over the chamber pot.'

'Has she eaten?'

'Cook took her dry toast and a long lecture for supper. Poor girl, she does look wretched. I hope I never end up in the family way.'

'If you were married, you might like children.'

'I can't see anyone wedding me. No, I'm going to be a famous actress instead.' Daisy grinned.

'Too big for here?'

'Oh, no, not now we've improved it. I'll always stay here. I'll just bring bigger crowds in.' She lifted a petticoat over Ava's head.

Hidden inside the folds of material, Ava took a deep breath. At least Daisy couldn't see her face for a moment; she was dreading having to tell her cast that they were potentially out of a home. Smoothing down the skirt, she pushed her arms into the dress and held her breath as Daisy pulled the buttons tight.

'It's looks lovely,' the girl said, stepping back.

Ava went over the mirror, skirts swishing the floorboards, and smiled. The dress yanked her in, showing a smooth, tiny waist before flaring up to her bosom. She couldn't breathe, admittedly, and would have to be careful to avoid eating more than a mouthful of soup, but hopefully Henry would like it. It was such a change from her usual print cotton working gowns. Would he think she looked like a lady?

'I'll put your hair up, miss,' Daisy said, dragging a stool over to the mirror and patting it for Ava to sit down.

Perched on the seat, she glanced in the mirror again. She wasn't vain normally, but she wasn't used to seeing herself dressed up for any reason other than acting. Her father hadn't been one for socialising and they'd spent their evenings in the parlour with the rest of the cast. She shivered and Daisy caught her hair up at the nape of her neck, twisting it into braids, which she pinned up on the back of her head.

'We need some seed pearl pins,' Daisy said.

'There isn't time to get any; Henry is waiting. I'll be wearing a hat when I arrive; that will have to do.'

Pushing plain pins into Ava's hair,

Daisy stepped back to admire her handiwork. 'Just think of you sitting with all those moneyed folks.'

'I'm trying not to think of that too much. I just hope I use the right fork and don't commit any terrible mistakes.'

'You'll be fine, miss. Just pretend you're acting the part of a lady in a play.'

'Well, I'm certainly doing that.'

Standing up, Ava touched her hair briefly to check it was firmly anchored. Daisy had done a good job. She tried breathing in cautiously and winced as a sharp pain dug into her ribs. She must remember to pull her skirt in when she sat down and perch on the edge of the chair, else she'd squash the bustle. No wonder ladies didn't do much; imagine trying to run a theatre trussed up like this every day! She'd stick to her light stays.

'Which shoes?' Daisy said.

'The satin slippers.'

'I'll go and get them; you go and

meet Mr Henry.'

Ava stepped through the door and clung to the banister as she shuffled down in her stocking feet, the wood cold beneath her toes, and her skirts tangling around her legs. Henry stood in the hall below, looking at the grandfather clock that stood by the door. She could picture him waiting for his soldiers with the same tight-lipped expression. Although then he wouldn't be wearing black evening dress, topped with a hat that made him appear even taller and broader across the shoulders.

'I'm here,' she said.

He turned around and smiled, then frowned as she walked from the dim light at the bottom of the stairs into the gas light of the hall.

'Is everything all right?' she said, moving back a step.

'You need to cover your shoulders, and . . . ' He nodded to her chest. 'That gown is lovely, but it's too low-cut for a dinner party.'

Heat flooded her face and she looked

down at the top of her breasts showing. Now he would think her a tart. She had been so pleased with the way she looked too, but already she'd made a mistake and she hadn't got out the door yet.

'You do look lovely,' he said, his voice softer. 'But I suspect the sight may be a little too much for the young men who will be joining us for dinner. It's best not to excite them too much and in that dress you look so tempting, they'll be fighting to hold up your music score.'

'But not the women,' she said.

'No, not them, I suspect. Look, here's Daisy. Daisy, could you get Miss Miller a piece of lace to put over her shoulders?'

'Of course, and her wrap; it'll be cold,' Daisy said, leaning down to put the slippers by Ava's feet.

'It's not an evening wrap,' Ava said, wiggling her feet into the shoes. 'Best leave it behind.'

'Leave it in the carriage; it's snowing out there,' Henry said.

191

Going to the front door, he opened it and whistled.

'Good luck, miss,' Daisy said, returning with the cloak and lace. 'I want to hear all about it in the morning.'

'I'll let you know every disaster,' Ava said, draping the lace across her shoulders and fastening the brooch. Swirling the wrap around her shoulders, she put on her hat and strode to the door, shivering as the icy wind met her. The horses huffed from the pavement outside. The coachman was wrapped up in a bright crimson box coat. Gas light reflected from the sparkling ice that coated the ground in glittering swirls.

'Take my arm,' Henry said, offering it.

It was warm under Ava's thin-sleeved dress, the wrap gaping open as she raised her elbow, her breath forming white clouds. The coachman jumped down and opened the door for her, stepping back and bowing. She smiled; it wasn't a reverence she was used to.

Henry held her arm tight as she climbed up the stairs into the carriage.

The coach seats were piled with thick rugs, warm to the touch. She nestled into the corner, placing her feet on a hot brick as Henry climbed in beside her and the coachman slammed the door shut. The gas lights flickered through the gaps in the blinds covering the window, casting shadows on the bench opposite. In the distance, shouts and laughter echoed down the street. Shivering, Ava tucked a blanket around her legs and wiggled her feet on the brick. It wasn't a night to be out in satin slippers.

'We're going to pick up Mrs Richards first,' Henry said, 'then go down to the house.'

She nodded. Luckily, in the dim coach he wouldn't be able to see her anxious frown. Her stomach clenched and she tried to breathe deep to relax, but the corset pulled around her chest, forcing her to sit upright. Why was she doing this? She could be seated by the fire at home, surrounded by her friends. It wasn't as if they had much time left together. Damn this corset — she needed fresh air!

Turning to the window, she yanked up the blind and tried to push the glass down.

'What are you doing? It's cold enough,' Henry said, catching her arm.

'I can't breathe.' She scrabbled at the glass, the tight underwear constricting her chest, suffocatingly tight. Sweating, she grabbed the handle — she had to get out of the coach.

'No, we're moving!' Henry slapped her hand down. 'What's the matter?'

Panting, she lay back against the seat, tears pricking her eyes. How foolish he must think her. The panic had gone, replaced by an icy chill that made her shudder.

'I couldn't get my breath,' she said.

'Sit up, let me loosen your corsets.'

'Not here!'

'Better here than at the dinner party, or when Mrs Richards joins us. She ignores a lot of things, but even she couldn't fail to notice that.' Reaching up, he knocked the coach roof. 'Stop for a moment please.'

'Henry, please.' She clutched the blanket close.

'You're not a fine lady yet.' He smiled, his teeth flashing in the shadows. Leaning across her, he pulled the blind down. 'Hold that blanket against you, but turn around and let me undo those ties before you faint.'

'I don't know what happened to me. I'm not usually one for fainting.' Holding the blanket against her front, she turned sideways on the seat. As wrong as it would be to have him undo her corset, she couldn't cope with the sharp pain under her ribs anymore and it would be more embarrassing to pass out upon entering her host's house. His fingers touched her back, sliding up her spine until they reached the top button of her dress. Although he must have been almost blind from the darkness, he unbuttoned them swiftly, his hands moving down smoothly and making her shiver.

'I don't think this is the first time you've undressed someone in a coach,' she said.

He chuckled and his hands stopped, then his lips touched the back of her bare neck. 'You are so tempting in that dress.'

'Even if I'm not a lady?'

'I don't want a lady.' He traced the line of her hair with her fingers and she trembled, heat rising to her skin as she turned her head to look at him over her shoulder. Tilting his head down, he kissed her mouth, his lips hard against hers, pressing firmly down as his arms encircled her.

She stiffened. What did he think she was? Jerking her head away, she sat up straight. 'Please finish dealing with the corset,' she said. 'It's cold.'

He brushed his lips against her neck once more, then his fingers deftly finished their work and she pulled herself upright as he undid the ties at the base of her corset and loosened the tapes.

'Is that better?' he said.

'Yes, thank you.'

She waited for him to touch her again, but he didn't. Instead he retied the ribbon and pulled the fabric of her dress back down to fasten it. His fingers fumbled this time, letting go of the tiny buttons.

'Have you enough light?' she said.

'I can do,' he said. His fingers stroked across her neck one last time, then he squeezed her shoulder with his hand. 'All done. Wrap yourself back up again.'

Ava shivered and then straightened without looking at Henry. It had been a bad idea to come out with him tonight; it could only make the situation between them more awkward.

9

'Was it a good night, miss?' Daisy said.

Ava turned around from her bedroom mirror as she pulled out the last of her hairpins. The dress she had worn to go out with Henry lay draped over the chair beside her, ready to go back into the costume storage. The garment hadn't been the latest fashion clearly, but it had been close enough not to raise too many eyebrows.

'Good night?' Ava echoed Daisy. 'Oh, yes, it was. Lots of dancing.'

She remembered the warmth of Henry's hand holding hers as they stepped out together. It had been a mistake to go with him; too intimate. It would be harder than ever now to stay away from him.

'How is Katie?' she said.

'Stopped vomiting, now eating non-stop. Cook ordered her out the kitchen.

Amelia's not so good — she found a bottle of cooking wine and drank the lot.'

Ava sighed and closed her eyes. The doctor had warned her that Amelia's fragile body could take no more alcohol.

'Has she been sick?'

'Not yet.'

'She'd better sleep in my room tonight in case she's ill during the night. Could you fetch her mattress?'

'Of course, miss. And I'll tell Cook to help Amelia up.'

'Thank you.'

Turning back to the looking-glass, Ava loosened her hair with her fingers so it fell down her back. A dark figure appeared behind her in the mirror reflection and she turned quickly.

'Clarence!' she said, heart beating fast. 'You startled me.'

He eyed her from the doorway, his gaze travelling the length of her body in a way that made her shiver. Reaching for her wrap, she flung it over her nightdress before turning to face him. The darkness in the hall cast shadows across his face.

'You spent the evening with Mr Scott-Leigh?' he said.

'Henry and I attended a dinner party together, along with an acquaintance of his.'

'The chaperone. I didn't see them with you when the carriage went past me in the street. In fact it looked rather like our parasitic guest was undressing you.'

Ava's cheeks burned. 'I had a problem with my gown.'

'Yes, I'm sure you did.'

She straightened her shoulders. 'It is none of your business, Clarence. I don't ask you what you get up to on the nights you stay away from The Orchid.'

'I'm trying to stop you making a total fool of yourself. Mr Scott-Leigh is only interested in one thing, and it's not your ability to run a theatre.' His lip curled. 'Or lack of ability.'

Ava stiffened. 'I'm not happy about

the way you are talking to me.'

'And I'm not happy watching you run around like a bitch in heat. I always thought we would marry and run The Orchid together, but you have cast me aside for a maimed solider.'

'Married? I would never have married you! You are my friend, or I thought you were.' Ava looked at his mouth, which was twisted in fury, then at the out-thrust jaw and clenched fists. She took a step back. 'I want you to leave my room, please.'

He stared at her, his chest rising and breath hissing between his teeth. She had never seen a man so close to losing total control.

'Please,' she said. 'Let's talk in the morning. It's late and we're both tired.'

Clarence stepped towards her, then the sound of footsteps came from the hall and Daisy's muffled voice drifted up the stairs.

'I must help them,' Ava said, keeping her voice light. 'Amelia isn't well.'

'She's a drain on all of us. I don't

know why you keep her here.'

Ava drew a sharp breath; Clarence had known Amelia for years. She looked at the open doorway, but didn't have the courage to walk past him.

There were footsteps on the steps.

'I've got Amelia,' Daisy called from the stairwell. 'And Cook has a mattress.'

'Bring her in, please,' Ava said, her shoulders relaxing.

Turning away from Clarence, she pushed her bed towards the wall to make space. Surely he would get the hint and leave? When she glanced carefully behind her, his malevolent shadow had vanished and she slumped down on her bed, muscles aching. What had happened to the boy she grew up with? Or had he always been this way and she had simply failed to see?

Daisy walked in with one arm around Amelia, who leaned against her. The sick girl's face was sunken and her eyes half-closed. Narrow, bony arms clutched Daisy.

'Here's her bed,' Cook said, dropping

a mattress on the floor. 'I've got a double sheet to put over it so she doesn't ruin it if she's sick.'

'I think she'll just sleep it off now,' Daisy said. 'In truth, considering how much she has drunk, she doesn't seem that bad.'

'Used to it,' Cook said, as she flicked the sheets out over the bed.

Ava turned to her wooden chest and pulled out spare blankets. When she came back to the bed, Amelia was already lying down, her face twisted to the side and a rattle coming from her lungs.

'It's not just the drink,' Cook said quietly.

'No,' Ava said, leaning down to tuck the blankets over the girl. Kneeling beside her, she touched the sharp-boned face and briefly closed her eyes as tears filled them. She had tried her best, but there had never been any hope for Amelia. She had been destroyed in her childhood by poverty and cruelty. No matter what kindness they had shown the girl, or any rich food they tried to feed her, her spirit had died many years before, taking with it any desire to live.

Ava cleared her throat. 'Thank you both. Now, go and get some sleep as we have a hard day tomorrow.'

'Rehearsing, miss?' Daisy said.

Ava remembered the letter about closing down The Orchid and swayed on her feet. What would happen to them all now? Suddenly exhausted, she pulled back the covers and climbed into her own bed.

'Do you need anything?' Daisy said, frowning. 'You look very pale.'

'I'm fine, just a little tired.'

'Good night, then. Call me if you need any help with Amelia. I'll leave the door open so I can hear you.' Daisy leaned down to adjust the sick girl's blankets before heading out of the room, Cook behind her.

Ava lay staring at the ceiling, nausea rising in her stomach. Clarence had to leave the theatre, but how could she sack him? The rest of her staff would never understand. She couldn't even ask him to go on the pretence of being unable to pay his wages, since he rarely claimed any.

Why had he stayed so long? She often skipped taking her salary herself, but she considered the theatre her own. Was that what Clarence also believed — that he had a claim to both The Orchid and to her? Certainly the arrival of Henry had changed him from a pleasant man into one who was jealous and vindictive. Or was this how he had been all along, and she had merely refused to see it? She had known for a long time about his visits to the brothels that lined the streets of London. They were, however, a common entertainment for unmarried young men, so she had ignored it.

He had lied about going, though, which left her wondering what else he had hidden. Sighing, she pushed down her bedcovers. Even though the night was cold, a film of sweat coated her skin. How much better she would feel if Henry were here to share her fears. What would it be like to sleep in his arms, cradled tightly to his body, letting his warmth and strength melt away her tension?

Ava turned abruptly over in bed. These were dangerous thoughts. She couldn't have Henry; and even if it could have worked between them, with Clarence's extreme reaction, it could be dangerous for Henry. He was from a family who liked to maintain their reputation, and she wouldn't put it past Clarence to spread rumours about Henry Scott-Leigh having an affair with an actress.

A cough came from the floor of her bedroom and Ava sat up. 'Amelia?' she said, softly.

The girl muttered and shifted on the mattress, then her breathing evened and Ava sat back, thankful. The girl's presence was strangely comforting, reminding her that she was not alone. She had managed without Henry until now and she would manage again. But would she ever be able to forget him?

★   ★   ★

'Miss? Miss? You have to wake up!'

'What?' she muttered. Her throat was dry and painful. She breathed in and choked, struggling to open her eyes, with her limbs feeling heavy, as if she had taken a dose of laudanum.

'Miss!'

The voice was urgent and Ava turned onto her side, blinking into the darkness. Her eyes stung and she coughed, then realised her nightgown was wet with sweat. Why was it so hot?

'Floor, get on the floor!' Amelia said.

A thin hand appeared at the side of the bed, reaching out to grip her.

Ava wriggled to the side of the mattress and dropped off onto the floorboards, landing with a thud on her hip. The air was clearer lower down and the fog in her mind lifted for a moment. She breathed in the acrid scent again.

Smoke. She clutched the other girl's hand tight, the fragile bones pressing against her palm. 'Can you crawl?' she said.

'I think so, miss.'

'Follow me. We have to get downstairs.' She breathed in sharply, coughing as the choking smoke filled her lungs. Which way was the door? The floorboards burned her hands and knees. What if they broke? She and Amelia could be sent plunging into the burning room beneath. Should she find the window instead and yell for help? In the middle of the night, would anyone be around to hear them?

'Miss?' Ameila started to cough, then retch.

Ava reached back, her hand grasping the other girl's shoulder. The smoke swirled again and she breathed sharply, choking as tears poured down her hot cheeks. A loud crack came from outside the room and she stiffened, frozen as waves of sheer terror hit her. For a brief moment she loosened her grip on

Amelia, the panic filling her mind with a primeval urge to race screaming down the stairs.

Instead, she squeezed the girl's shoulder and opened her mouth to speak, but the smoke swirled and she closed it again. Leaning down, Ava pulled off the woollen stockings she wore under the nightgown and tied one around her mouth. It acted as a rough filter and she drew in tiny breaths. Tying the second around Amelia's face, she crawled across the floor to the door.

The floorboards were hotter here, searing the skin of her knees, and she winced. Stretching up her arm, she grasped the door handle. Agonising pain shot across her palm and she groaned against the gag tight across her mouth, teeth biting into the fabric as she wrenched her hand away, tearing the skin from her palm.

'Miss?' Amelia said, coughing.

Ava looked behind her. The girl lay on the floor, eyes half-closed, face pale; she wouldn't survive much longer. Ava pulled the wool from her mouth.

'Amelia, you must get up!' she said. 'I can't carry you; I'm not strong enough.'

Amelia couldn't die now, not like this! She had to get the girl out. Wrapping the hem of her nightgown around her hand, Ava twisted the door handle again, tears filling her eyes as the hot metal burned into her hand. Then the door clicked open, bringing a rush of heat and smoke into the room.

Reaching back, Ava grasped Amelia's hand and pulled her hard. Amelia groaned and struggled, trying to lie back down.

'Come on,' Ava pleaded. Turning, she stared into the dark corridor. Where was everyone? Why had no one come to help? Were they already dead in their own beds?

'I can't move,' Amelia said.

'Then since I cannot leave you, we will both die.'

'No, you go!'

'I'm not leaving you.'

'Go, miss, go. There's no hope for

me. There was never any hope for me.' Amelia coughed violently, retching again.

'Come on!' Ava grasped the girl's arm and pulled hard. Amelia moved onto her hands and knees, shuffling forward a few paces.

'Follow me,' Ava said.

Tightening the filter around her mouth, she crawled out through the door and onto the dark landing. Black smoke swirled up the stairs, masking the ceiling with thick tendrils. Dizzy, she shook her head. Which way was it? The carpet was hot and rough under her burnt knees. Moving forward, the floor fell away beneath her and she screamed, sliding down the stairs.

Ava landed halfway down the steps, winded and coughing. She looked up towards the landing. 'Roll yourself down, Amelia,' she pleaded.

Amelia toppled down the stairs, her body dropping past Ava with a sickening thud. The smoke swirled again and Ava dropped her head to the floor, black spots floating in front of her eyes. Where was Amelia?

A hand grasped her leg and she instinctively kicked.

'Ava, it's me,' Henry's voice came through the smoke.

'Where's Amelia?'

'I don't know. But come with me now, before the stairs burn though.'

The dark spots swirled in front of her eyes again and her head fell against the steps. She couldn't survive much longer without air. But where was Amelia?

The tug on her leg came again, sharp and insistent. Ava opened her eyes briefly, then dropped her head back down. She couldn't move; it was too exhausting. Better to stay here.

A hard grip grasped her thighs, pulling her down the stairs, scraping carpet burns across her cheeks. She groaned, faintly aware of being carried, of a blast of fresh air and the hard sensation of someone slapping her face, before the darkness took her again.

* * *

The ground was cold beneath Ava and her clothes were wet. Opening her eyes, she looked up into a black sky, then retched violently, twisting her head to the side.

A soft, damp cloth wiped her cheek and mouth. 'Miss?' Daisy said.

Ava coughed, vomiting again.

'It's all right, miss. The doctor said you'd likely be sick.'

'Amelia?' Ava said, 'Henry?'

'They're looking for Amelia.' Daisy's voice broke. 'And Henry's been taken in the ambulance to the hospital. It was the bullet in his spine — it moved.'

Ava groaned, her muscles spasming as pain hit her. She couldn't have lost both of them. Please, no! Gulping for air, she opened her stinging eyes. 'Katie and Walter? Cook?'

'All safe — they got out via the kitchen. We can't find Clarence, though the firemen are searching.'

Ava remembered his dark, angry eyes

as he stared at her and shivered. Clarence hated her. How far would he go for vengeance? Surely he wouldn't burn down The Orchid? It had been his only home. No, she must be wrong.

Daisy stood up, a hand to her mouth. 'They've found Amelia,' she said.

Ava turned her head. A fireman had crawled out of the main doors, dragging a prone figure behind him. As the girl's body jerked, then dropped still, hot tears filled Ava's eyes. Amelia had been right — there had never been any hope for her. But she hadn't deserved to die like this.

'Help me up, Daisy,' she said.

'You must lie still.'

Ava tried to pull herself up, nausea rising in her throat again. Twisting sideways, she moved onto her hands and knees and tried to crawl.

'Stay where you are, miss,' the fireman said. 'I'll bring her over.'

Leaning down, he lifted Amelia and carried her over, with a care and protectiveness that the girl had rarely experienced in life. Laying her on the ground, he put his coat over her, then dragged a hand down his face. 'Such a young lass,' he said.

Ava knelt beside the prone figure and reached out to stroke the soot-blackened face. Amelia's skin was warm and Ava drew a sharp breath. Did the girl still live? But her chest lay still under the fireman's coat and her eyes stared upwards, unseeing.

'I should have got her out,' she said, voice breaking. 'I let her die.'

'Amelia didn't have the strength. She was too ill, miss,' Daisy said, reaching out to pull the coat over the blank eyes. Then putting her hands over her face, the young actress sobbed.

Ava laid a hand on her back, dropping her head forward as tears flowed from her own eyes, falling in black, sooty spots on her torn night-gown. What caused this disaster? And how was Henry? Did he live? Coughing, she struggled to her feet and clutched at a low wall, doubling over. 'I must get to the hospital,' she said.

'That's a good idea, madam.' The fireman took her arm. 'Let's get you there.'

'Not for me. I must see how Henry is.'

'Of course, and you can see him whilst being treated yourself. That's a nasty burn you have on your hand there.'

Ava looked down at her palm, remembering the closed bedroom door. Surely it had been left open by Cook and Daisy? Had Amelia closed it? It seemed unlikely in her drunken state.

'Do you know what caused the fire?' she said, looking at the fireman.

'Not yet. Stray candle, or unbanked fire? These old theatres go up in flames all the time. Dangerous places, really.'

Ava turned her head to look at The Orchid. Hoses snaked into the building and a thick plume of dark smoke poured from the roof.

'Did you find Clarence?' she said.

'No, but he might still be in the

kitchen, or have escaped from the passageway the other side. We mustn't lose hope.'

'You won't find him,' she said, half to herself. 'He'll be miles away by now.'

'What, miss?'

She shook her head and coughed again, retching. The fireman put his arm around her shoulders.

'Hospital for you, miss! And no more arguments.'

Ava rested against the wall as the man hailed a cab and spoke to the driver. She shivered violently, pain spreading up her arm from her burnt hand. Her gaze returned to Amelia, and then Daisy who sat sobbing beside the prone figure, before she looked again at the charred remains of The Orchid. She had lost everything now — her home, her family, and maybe even the man she loved.

10

Seated beside Henry's bed, Ava stared at her bandaged hand, the white wraps bright against her soot-covered dress. The nurses had wanted her to go straight home after the wound had been dressed, but she'd refused. She glanced at Henry again. His face was pale against the crisp pillow case, the narrow iron bed hardly large enough to contain his tall and muscular frame. She couldn't leave him now. And she didn't have anywhere to go to.

If only he would open his eyes! But since his return from theatre — an ordeal she could scarcely contemplate without shuddering — he had remained unconscious. Was it the chloroform? The nurse had warned her it could be dangerous. Sniffing, she grimaced. The sweet scent of the chemical still lingered on him, and mixed with the smell of soot, made her stomach clench. How long had she sat here now? Three, four hours? Surely he should be coming around now?

The sharp sound of a nurse's shoes hitting the wooden floorboards echoed down the long ward and Ava lifted her head. Under her starched white cap, the nurse's lips were pressed tight together as she paused by Henry's bed.

'Has he shown any signs of moving?' the nurse said.

Ava winced. 'None.' Her gaze dropped to Henry's face again and she squeezed his hand as if she could will him back into life. She couldn't lose him now. What did it matter if society frowned on them? She loved him!

The nurse made a note on a chart she carried, then looked at Ava and frowned. 'You must go home, Miss Miller. You can scarcely stand yourself.'

'I can't leave him.' Ava looked at his prone figure. She had left Amelia and the girl had died. There was no chance of her letting Henry down too. What if she returned tomorrow and found his bed empty? Surely he could sense her presence? Tears filled her eyes and she bowed her head to hide them, then broke into sobs as a warm and kind hand rested on her shoulder.

'My dear, there is nothing you can do. And visiting time ended a while ago. You really have to leave so we can do our job. Mr Scott-Leigh will be well cared for. Have you informed his family that he is here?' the nurse said.

His family? Ava straightened, remembering the letter. Hysterical laughter bubbled in her throat — Felix Scott-Leigh couldn't shut The Orchid down now. What would happen to them all? They could hardly act from the ruins of the theatre, standing amongst the burned beams and charred ashes like the survivors of Pompeii. Dropping her head into her hands, she moaned. She was deeply in debt and had no means to pay it off.

Then her gaze returned to the still figure in front of her and she drew a deep breath. She could bear all of it, even debtors' gaol, if only Henry were all right.

'Miss,' the nurse said gently. 'You really must leave now. We need to settle the patients for the night.'

Ava rose slowly to her feet, glancing out of the large windows at the approaching dusk. Evening had arrived without her knowledge. In fact, the whole day had passed in a blur. She ought to be back at the theatre taking charge, directing her actors, seeing what could be salvaged from the wreckage. Arranging for Amelia to be buried. But she could think of nothing except the man in front of her and her grief for the young girl she had failed to save.

Her chest tightened and she grasped the back of her chair for support as terror spread through her body. Had she caused this terrible tragedy by leading Clarence on? Without the fake engagement, which he had taken so seriously, would he have turned into the monster that he had become? Because she was in no doubt that he had started the fire. His body had not been recovered from the ruins, his charred face not spotted escaping from the building. In her mind again she saw his eyes, dark with hate and resentment.

In Clarence's furious mind, she was responsible for everything that was wrong with his life. Thinking of his twisted face, she shuddered. Thank goodness she had never been tempted to wed him — marriage to a man such as he would have been purgatory. Once the initial period had worn off, she would have become his whipping boy for his every frustration until by stealth or vindictive behaviour, he would have wrested control of The Orchid from her.

Inside his black mind, Clarence didn't love her; he hated her because she represented everything that he wanted to be — popular with the staff, a skilled director, and in charge of the theatre. He would have controlled her every move, until she broke down and became a shell of herself — a living ghost desperate to perform his every whim.

No, it wasn't love her childhood friend had felt for her, but jealousy, and he had been nurturing it for years behind that smiling exterior.

Shivering, she looked at Henry's still face. First Amelia, then Henry. Who else would pay the price for Clarence's vengeance? Leaning down, she laid a hand on the still leg of the man in the bed before her.

'I love you,' she whispered.

His face remained passive and she raised a hand to wipe her eyes, then taking a deep breath, she walked slowly up the ward.

* * *

Under winter rain, the charred beams of The Orchid glistened like exposed, wet tree roots. Ava tilted her head to gaze up at the gaping hole where the roof had fallen in, leaving the top of the red brick walls exposed. Swirls of white smoke still drifted through the ruins, filling her lungs once again with the acid scent of death. Coughing, she stepped back.

'It's horrible,' Daisy said from behind her. 'And poor, poor Amelia.'

'What's going to happen to us?' Katie said.

Ava turned quickly. 'You shouldn't be here, Katie. It's not good for you.'

'I couldn't stay away.' The girl's mouth trembled, then she broke out into harsh sobs. 'It was my home too!'

'Of course it was.' Ava put her arm around the shaking girl, wincing at the pain in her hand.

'Let me.' Walter took Katie instead, placing a hand across her shoulders. 'We're all going to stick together — share our money until we get jobs.'

'What money?' Daisy said. 'I've got a nightgown and a coat. Not even shoes.' She raised the edge of the chemise to show her blue feet.

'Oh, Daisy — and you, Katie, as well.

I never noticed.' Ava's hands went to the second-hand dress the hospital had lent her.

'No, miss!' Daisy said. 'The world can't see you standing in the street in your corset!'

'It is unfortunate we are all without relatives,' Walter said. 'There are times when you need family.'

'We have friends,' Katie said. 'Come on, Daisy, let's go to Drury Lane. I bet they'd be able to lend us some frocks.'

'I'd better accompany you both,' Walter said. 'Considering what you are wearing.' Reaching over, he laid a hand gently on Ava's elbow. 'Come with us?' She shook her head. 'My darling girl, you're exhausted and injured. Please come and find somewhere to rest.'

'What did the fireman do with . . . ?' She sniffed loudly.

'They have taken Amelia to the under-takers, from where we can arrange a funeral.' The grip tightened and the older man cleared his throat painfully. 'I knew she wouldn't be with us much longer, but did she have to suffer so? Poor little girl, a hard end for one who suffered so much in life.'

'I couldn't save her.'

'Of course you couldn't. We'd have lost you, too, without Henry. He went back in when the firemen refused to enter.'

'And he has paid a heavy price for his bravery.'

'There is always hope, Ava.'

She remembered the silent figure in the hospital bed. How desperately she wanted to be back there.

Walter squeezed her arm. 'You can't help anyone unless you rest yourself. Come to Drury Lane; our friends will help us.'

Ava looked at the charred ruins in front of her again. 'Henry's father was arriving today to close us down.'

'I suspect he'll have other concerns. Does he know yet about his son?'

'I sent a telegram to the house and to the family's lawyers. Mr Scott-Leigh will arrive in the city to bad news.' Ava closed her eyes at the thought of the terrible shock that awaited him. 'I should wait for him,' she said. 'Offer my support.'

'I suspect that's the last thing he will want, and you can't take much more.'

Ava drew a deep breath, then doubled over, coughing. The dark spots were dancing again in front of her eyes and her muscles were stiff and painful. Despite the gown change, her hair and body reeked of smoke. The dark, healing oblivion of sleep was all she desired now.

'Come, now,' Walter said.

Like a small child, she clung to his arm as he led her down the street to the glowing lights of the Drury Lane Theatre. Outside the famous white, square building, a long queue of theatre-goers snaked around the door and up the ice-covered road. Ava lowered her head to avoid the stares as she stepped past them, following Walter to the stage door at the back. White clouds emerged from her mouth as she panted for breath, and shivering, she rubbed her arms.

Walter knocked on the door. 'I assume the girls must already be inside,' he said.

'Hope so,' Ava said. London in the evening wasn't the place for two young girls dressed in nightgowns. If they only got away with a pinched bottom they would be doing well.

The door opened, sending a welcome spike of light and heat across the dark pavement. 'Ava, my love, come in. Daisy and Katie are here. They told me what happened.'

Ava looked up. It was her old friend, John Stephens. A lead actor of Drury Lane, he had been a long-standing friend of her father's. She remembered the evenings she had spent with them both in the parlour, the air filled with the comforting scent of their pipes. Tears filled her eyes and she lowered her head to hide them. If only her father was here now.

'Ava, come in, darling,' John said. He

took her hand, then dropped it when she gasped. 'You're hurt!' he said.

'It is only minor.' She looked at him. 'We have lost Amelia and likely Henry Scott-Leigh. The Orchid has burned to the ground.'

The words tumbled from her lips. Spoken quickly, as if in her haste, she could lessen their pain. Then her throat tightened, and pressing her hands to her face, she sobbed desperately, shoulders heaving, a burning feeling blocking her lungs as if she was back in the deadly smoke once more.

A strong arm went around her back, and she drew a shuddering breath as John swung her up into his arms, his hand under her knees.

'Take her to the dressing rooms,' Walter said.

★ ★ ★

Ava opened her eyes and stared at the unfamiliar ceiling. Why wasn't she in her bedroom? Then the tears came again and she lay still on the unfamiliar mattress.

A wet flannel dabbed her face and she turned her head. Daisy sat beside the couch, face pale and eyes damp. 'We're in our new lodgings,' the girl said. 'Walter carried you. You've been asleep for over a day.'

Ava jerked up. 'Lodgings? We have no money for rent!'

'Don't worry about the money, miss. Drury Lane has given work to Walter and me. Mr Stephen's pulled strings. It's only bit parts, but enough to cover a room for us three. Walter's going to stay with friends, since he can't share with three women.'

Ava dropped back and looked around the room, a frown creasing her forehead. It was a large, square chamber with white-washed walls. The bed she lay on was a double, covered by several blankets. Opposite her, a fire burned in the range behind a wooden kitchen table, sending clouds of smoke up the chimney. Looking at them, she shuddered. 'Where is Katie?' she said.

'In the market; we need food.'

Ava closed her eyes. It seemed strange that her actors had taken control of the situation. She had spent so long looking after them, when they were clearly very capable of looking after themselves. Her cheeks warmed. Had she been too controlling, assuming that she always knew what was best for them?

A door banged and Katie hurried into the room, a basket hanging from her arm. 'Miss, you're awake!' she cried, smiling. 'How are you feeling?'

'Better, thank you.' Ava sat up, pushing the covers down.

'Stay there until you've eaten something.' Katie put the basket on the table and unpacked it: a packet of tea, loaf of bread, bottle of milk, eggs, carrots, and a bloodstained wrapped parcel that looked to contain beef. Taking a saucepan from the range, Katie emptied in the packet of meat, then picked up a knife to slice the carrots.

'Soup, I thought,' she said.

'I must go to the hospital,' Ava said.

'I called in to see him on my way home,' Katie said. 'His father is there, so I wouldn't go over yet. He looked grim. The nurse told me that Henry isn't in pain and has blinked his eyes. That's a good sign, isn't it? The nurse sounded pleased.'

Daisy clasped her hands. 'I have been praying for him. We have already lost Amelia and Clarence. I do so hope that Mr Scott-Leigh will be well. He is such a kind man.'

'Clarence?' Ava said. 'Lost Clarence?'

Daisy stiffened. 'I'm sorry, miss. I thought you knew! There's no sign of him. He must have been trapped inside.'

'I thought I saw him,' Katie said, sounding puzzled. 'In the waiting room outside Mr Henry's room. But when I turned around to look, he'd gone. I suppose it was just someone wearing the same coat.'

'Maybe you were just hoping?' Daisy said.

Katie frowned. 'I don't feel so sorry about him, not like I do over Amelia and Mr Henry.' She clapped a hand to her mouth and stared at Ava.

'Why don't you feel so sorry?' Ava said gently.

Katie swallowed. 'He could be mean sometimes, when you weren't there. And he told me he hoped the baby would die because it had brought shame on you and The Orchid.'

Ava looked at Daisy. 'What was he like to you?'

The girl shrugged. 'He hardly spoke to me, except during rehearsals. Then he could get nasty if I made a mistake.'

'He bruised your arm once, didn't he, Dais?' Katie said, scooping up the carrots and flinging them into the saucepan.

'I forgot my lines twice and he got angry.' Daisy drew a sharp breath. 'It was scary — his face went still and blank, but his eyes were narrow and filled with anger.'

Ava remembered Clarence's expression when he came into her room. It had been the same controlled, suppressed fury that Daisy was describing. What resentments burned inside his mind to create such rage? 'Maybe it is for the best that he has gone,' she said. Swinging her feet to the floor, she glanced at the two girls. Dressed in borrowed outfits, their faces were smeared with smuts.

'What's going to happen now, miss?' Daisy said, her voice low. 'The theatre has gone, hasn't it?'

Ava sighed. 'We would have lost it anyway. Henry's father had ordered it to be shut down.'

'I doubt he was expecting to see it shut down quite so permanently,' Katie said.

Ava smiled grimly. Mr Scott-Leigh would indeed be shocked when he saw his theatre. Would he blame her for it? Might he be right to? Had her poor handling of Clarence led to this disaster and the death of poor Amelia? She pushed thoughts of Henry from her mind. She couldn't yet contemplate his death.

It had all been going so well. Even though the reviews of the new play had been mixed, she had been certain it would make them money. But now there was no theatre to put on the play they had thought would save them. Ava blinked back tears again as she remembered the much-loved theatre that had been her home her whole life. She had never been able to consider leaving The Orchid, but now there was nothing of it left. Everything she owned had been lost in the flames. Would she now face debtors' gaol?

A loud clatter came from the table as Katie put three bowls and spoons down. 'Soup's ready,' she said.

Daisy looked at Ava, the younger girl's face streaked with the same tears that she knew ran down her own.

'We'll be all right,' Ava said, reaching out for her hand.

'We'll stick together, miss, like we always have. You're not going to desert us now?'

'Of course not.'

Daisy nodded and wiped her eyes. 'I always wanted to be on the stage at Drury Lane. I dreamt of it. But now it's happened, I don't want it. It's that famous saying, isn't it? Be careful what you wish for, as it might come true. I wished for fame and the lights of the West End, but I never expected it to come at such a terrible price.'

Ava nodded. She had wished for Henry to leave. And now he lay broken and wounded in a hospital, and she had to explain to his father what had happened to both his son and the theatre he owned.

The sound of soup splashing into bowls distracted her, even though her stomach clenched in revulsion at the thought of food. In their current situation she couldn't refuse a meal, as it was impossible to tell when they might have another. She had just joined the great crowd of London paupers.

Daisy brought a dish of beef soup over. Dipping the spoon into the thick broth, Ava swallowed a mouthful, her smoke-damaged throat burning. Putting down the bowl, she rubbed her neck and looked at the two girls, who had huddled around the small fire.

'When are you at work, Daisy?' she said.

'Tonight. It's a non-speaking part, but next week the director said I can have some lines.'

'I wish I could work at Drury Lane,' Katie said.

Ava's gaze dropped to the girl's stomach. The bulge was hidden behind a voluminous apron, but soon it would be visible no matter what Katie wore. She was a slim girl. Would the landlord throw them out when the pregnancy was discovered? It was common with unmarried mothers. Why did Katie have to get herself into this state?

Then thinking of Henry, she sighed. If Henry had invited her into his bed, would she have refused? The temptation to touch him, feel his arms around her was so overwhelming, it was possible she could have ended up in the same state as the young actress. Thankfully the situation had never arisen, since Henry's morals were clearly so much higher than her own. He would never have entertained such an idea.

'We will have to find a midwife soon, Katie,' Ava said.

Katie lowered her spoon. 'Can we afford it? With Mr Henry in hospital, there will be no one to pay for the foster care.'

Ava stiffened. The girl was right. How could they support a baby now, when they could barely pay for themselves? Walter and Daisy alone couldn't support five of them, even assuming they would always be willing to share their wages. Circumstances changed all the time; they both might meet someone they owed a higher level of duty to.

'You can have my money,' Daisy said. 'And I know Walter will offer too.'

'Your wages only just cover the rent here,' Katie said, hunching over her soup. 'I've been such a stupid girl!' Her eyes filled with tears. 'Whatever was I thinking of? He wasn't worth it; he cared nothing for me! Now I'm causing nothing but trouble for you all.'

Ava looked at the girl's pale face and remembered the rushing and deadly Thames, speeding through the centre of the city yards away. So many girls in Katie's situation ended up in those dark, cold waters.

'We will manage,' she said firmly. 'I promise. As soon as my lungs clear, I'll get work too. I'm sure Drury Lane will be able to fit me in somewhere. They have asked me to work for them before. With the three of us working, we'll be able to support you and the baby. Someone needs to take care of the house anyway. We can't all go out to work, else there'll be no meals or clean clothes.'

'But I'm no good at household chores! I've never ironed in my life.'

'Then you will learn.' Closing her eyes, Ava rested back against the wall, waves of weariness hitting her. A life of washing and scrubbing would never fit with Katie, but as long as the girl had a roof over her head and food in her belly, she'd have to accept it as her lot for now. Once the child was born, they could take turns working. Gazing around the single chamber, she sighed. Was this where she would spend the remainder of her life — sharing close quarters with her girls, whilst Walter lodged down the street? After years of running her own establishment, it was a hard fall to take. But at least it wasn't debtors' gaol. Yet.

Swallowing the last of her soup, Ava put the bowl down. 'I'm going to the hospital to check on Mr Scott-Leigh. Keep the door closed, unless it's Walter or anyone else you know.'

'Yes, miss,' Daisy said. 'Will you take a cab to the hospital? It's a long way to walk.'

Ava shook her head. The days of calling cabs were over.

* * *

Henry focused on the voice again. It came from a distance, muffled. A man's voice. Twitching his head, he parted his swollen eyelids and looked straight into the flushed, tight-lipped face of his father. Struggling, Henry opened his eyes wider. Where was he? And what had happened to Ava? He remembered her terrified face, surrounded by smoke and flames. Had she got out? His mouth formed her name.

'What?' his father said, leaning over.

'Ava?' The sound was choked, emerging from Henry's damaged lungs. A sharp pain flared across his back and he winced.

'Ava? Miss Miller? Why are you interested in her?' his father said. 'Damn girl bankrupted my theatre, then burned it down! Almost killing you in the process.'

'Is she alive?'

'I have no idea.'

Footsteps echoed down the ward,

241

stopping at his bed. Henry opened his eyes again, blinking as his vision blurred. A familiar figure stood at the end of his bed.

'Ava,' he said. 'Ava.' He tried to lift his hand towards her.

She quickly stepped past his father and stood beside his pillow. Tears fell from her face onto his white bed linen.

'I feared you were lost,' she said, her voice breaking as she reached for his hand. 'I couldn't bear the thought of losing you.'

Henry squeezed her hand, then stiffened as her warm touch was roughly pulled away.

'So instead of working at the business, you've been carrying on with a theatre girl!' his father snapped.

Henry tightened his lips. The days when he paid attention to his father's wishes were long gone. He reached for Ava's hand again.

'I'd be careful, Henry,' his father said. 'You have a hole in your spine and medical care is expensive.'

'Are you threatening me?'

'I'm telling you the facts. Who is going to look after you if you end up paralysed? Because there's a good chance you might. This girl? Is she going to push you around in a bath-chair? It that a life you would inflict upon her?'

'How dare you!' Ava said. 'If I want to spend my life caring for your kind, wonderful son, then I will.'

Henry tried to move his legs. They lay still under the bedclothes. Fisting up his hand, he banged it on his thigh, but felt nothing. Had the doctors said he would never walk again? He'd faced that bleak future when he had been originally injured, and the time he had spent in the hospital had done nothing to disabuse him of how hard a life without legs would be. He couldn't have Ava caring for him; it was no life for her and he loved her too much to do it to her. He let go of her hand and tried to straighten his shoulders.

Damn, he couldn't even pull himself up on the pillows. Coughing, he lay back, exhausted.

'Let me help,' Ava said.

'Don't touch him, you might make his injury worse,' his father said. 'You clearly know nothing about wounds, girl. What type of nurse would you make? He needs specialist care and that comes at a price. How are you going to pay for that? Henry has no means of his own.'

'You would cast me off because you disapprove of my choice of bride?' Henry said. Beside him, Ava gave a sharp intake of breath. 'Who else, Father, would take on a man who couldn't walk? What burden would I be to you then?'

'At least I would avoid the sniggering of my friends, knowing that my son had taken up with an actress piece and one whose morals have long been under question. What effect would that have on my businesses? No, you will come home.'

Henry looked at his father, recognising the hard set to his mouth. He was a man who lacked compassion and caring, as did his mother. They would continue their selfish, work-obsessed existence whilst he would be left to wheel himself about the house and stay away from society as if his injury could be contagious.

'I have friends who would help me,' Henry said, raising his chin.

'They would help at first, then you would become a burden. Long-term illness is irritating for those who are well.'

'Maybe for you it is,' Ava said. 'Not for all. I have cared for many sick people and never found it a burden.'

'But a sick husband? One never able to father your children, or support you? That is a different issue.'

'I would still do it willingly.'

The sunlight from the window caught Ava's hair, sending pale streaks through it that for a moment aged her. Henry closed his eyes. What life could he offer her? His father was right, he couldn't let her spend her years caring for him. They wouldn't even be able to afford a nurse to take on some of the burden. He had little income of his own.

Ava didn't even have a home anymore; she had lost her beloved theatre. She had her friends to care for and Katie's baby due soon. So many heavy burdens rested on those slim shoulders that he couldn't add to them.

Henry closed his eyes. 'I need specialist treatment if I am ever going to walk again.'

'Of course, Henry . . . ' Ava said.

'And I cannot pay for it,' he admitted.

'We can . . . ' She stopped.

'You can what?' his father said. 'Care for him in debtors' gaol? I know your debts, Ava Miller. If you can't repay your creditors, that's where you will end up. And what will happen to my son then? Left to die in a workhouse?'

'No!' she cried.

'Father! Do not be so callous!' Henry said.

'Face up to the truth then, son. You are helpless and need the family money. This talk of staying together is absurd. How long will your love last under that type of pressure? Even if it is love, which I doubt, I know the theatre type, and Miss Miller here would drop you like a hot coal once you were penniless.'

'I would not!'

'Ava, please.' Henry held up a hand. A sharp, burrowing pain gnawed in his back and his vision clouded at the edges. Thirst burned his throat and his eyes half-closed.

'I have to stay here for now, probably for a long time. Decisions can be made later,' he said.

'Please, Henry,' Ava said, 'don't leave me.'

He squeezed her hand and swallowed the hard lump in his throat. How could he get through the day without her? Each morning he woke up, she was the first thing he thought of. It was impossible to imagine his life without her in it. Now that he knew what it meant to truly love someone, being separated from her would be agony. But it would be worse to watch her dying a little inside each day — married to an invalid, unable to have a family of her own. He couldn't inflict such a life on her. He loved her too much.

Henry let go of her hand. 'You need to take care of your friends,' he said.

Ava stared at him, her mouth open and eyes filling with tears. Smudges of black soot still stained her cheek and he fought the urge to wipe them away. She must think him a traitor, selling his feelings for her in exchange for an easier life.

'Henry,' she said, her voice hoarse.

He shook his head. 'You must go now. You have other responsibilities.'

'I'm not going to leave you here injured.'

Henry took a deep breath. Ava would never walk out on someone because they were sick or hurt, he knew that about her. In order for her to leave, he would have to be cruel.

'Ava, I appreciate what you did for The Orchid, but there is nothing left for us to work on. The theatre has burned down and there is no further need for us to work together. My father will pay the remaining wages of the staff and arrange for the lawyers to sort out the insurance claim.'

'Wages?' his father said.

'Wages,' Henry said firmly. 'They have lost their jobs and homes through no fault of their own.'

Ava gave a small sniff, then raised her chin high. 'If I am of no further use, I will return to Drury Lane.'

Henry nodded. She had told him where she would be in the hope he might follow her. But he couldn't. It would be heartless to condemn her to a life of poverty and worry. He had seen her on the stage; she was a fine actress and would find work. But she would never run her own theatre again and without family, would be reliant on her friends for support.

His fist clenched. How would she manage in the dangerous world of London's poor? Could he persuade his father to take care of her? He glanced at the man standing beside the bed, but drew a sharp breath at the look his fury he was directing towards Ava. Did he blame her for the loss of the theatre? It was only money that drove his father on. Rather than asking him to help Ava, he would be better ensuring that they didn't come into contact. The man could be vindictive when his will was thwarted.

'Shall I leave then?' Ava said.

Henry winced, then swallowed the lump in his throat. He raised his hand, desperate to beg her to stay, to love him in the manner he loved her.

'Henry?' she said.

He couldn't do it to her. She deserved so much better than the life he could offer her. 'You should return to your friends,' he said. 'They need you.'

'And you do not?'

He closed his eyes. Why did this have to be so hard? Why were her eyes staring so deeply into his, twisting his heart and causing his skin to burn? Finally he had met a woman he loved, but she could never be his. 'No,' he said. 'I do not. I have my family.'

'And money,' she said, her voice hard.

'And money.' He forced himself to gaze back at her, willing himself not to give way when the tears spilled onto her cheeks.

Ava whirled around and strode down the aisle of the ward towards the door. With one hand on the handle, she paused and looked back at him; but when he remained silent, she flung the door open and fled outside, slamming it behind her.

Henry slumped against the pillows, a violent pain spreading up his back, as if even his body had revolted against his decision. However, there was no other choice. He loved her enough to let her go, to find happiness with another man who could read and walk. Who could earn enough to be independent.

'Good,' his father said.

'Can you leave me alone, please?' Henry said.

Mr. Scott-Leigh snatched his coat from the bed and strode out of the ward. Henry watched him go. He didn't want the man, to whom he had never been close, standing beside him at this time. It was so frustrating that he couldn't defy his father and take his own route in life, but with no means of earning a living he was completely trapped. Damn that bullet! Was he to be condemned to be forever a burden? To have to be eternally grateful to people for their assistance? What life would that be?

Could he apply to a soldiers' hospital and pay over his meagre pension in return for food and lodgings? It wouldn't be the life he would have chosen, but at least he could be free from his family. Did it matter how he lived, now he had lost Ava?

Henry shuffled on the bed and tried to move his legs again. Nothing, just a sharp pain in his back. Was he really paralysed? He looked up as the sound of footsteps echoed down the ward. It was the doctor, flanked by nurses, and they were coming towards his bed.

'Mr Scott-Leigh,' the doctor said, looking at his chart.

'How bad is it?' Henry said.

'We took out the bullet, but there could be some damage to the spinal cord.'

'Will I walk again?'

'It's too early to tell. You need bed rest until the wound has healed. That could take several weeks, but your lungs should clear in the next few days. Try not to cough too much in case it aggravates the back injury.'

Henry nodded, aware of his throat tickling. It seemed that for the time being, his life would be spent flat on his back in hospital. How had everything gone so wrong in such a short space of time?

Ava stumbled back to the lodgings, her vision blinded by tears. A carriage flew past her, splashing dirty water up her dress. Putting her hands over her face, she sobbed. It had been so wonderful to see Henry awake, his eyes staring into hers. Then he had rejected her because she wasn't rich enough to care for him! Why did it always come back to money? Did the click of coins have to haunt her life so? She didn't care about luxuries or fine gowns. Her cash went on supporting those she loved and who depended on her. But if she hadn't been responsible for so many others, would Henry have stayed with her?

Ava wiped her sleeve across her eyes and took a deep breath to control her sobs. Her lungs were painful and she coughed sharply, leaning against a shop wall to steady herself. She had lost her father, Amelia, her home, and now Henry. What else could be taken away from her? There was so little left.

Closing her eyes, she pictured the Thames in her mind — the cool, dark waters — and imagined them closing over her head as she sank into peaceful oblivion.

No! She thumped a fist against the wall, grazing her knuckles. That was no way to think! What about Daisy and Katie? How would they manage without her? She had responsibilities to her friends who needed and loved her, as she did them. But why was it her heart that had to be left broken? Was she destined to spend her life looking after other people, with no one to hold her tight and whisper that they loved her?

Bowing her head, she sobbed, not caring about the surprised glances of passers-by. If only she could turn back time and be in her bedroom in The Orchid with Henry sleeping in the spare room and Amelia, poor Amelia, on her mattress. Would the girl have survived if she had slept in the other bedroom with Daisy and Katie? The fire must have been started outside her own room, as that was where the flames had been most ferocious. Clarence had meant to kill her.

Straightening, she wiped her eyes and leaned back against the stone wall. Where was Clarence? Would he try again if he knew she had survived? Or had he punished her enough now for her crime of falling in love with another man? Katie said she had spotted the assistant manager at the hospital, or thought she had.

There was no proof to take to the police. It might be worth talking to them though, since they could look out for him, especially if she mentioned that Henry Scott-Leigh might be at risk. Ava coughed and held a handkerchief to her mouth. There was nothing she could do about Amelia or Henry, but she could find Clarence. Until he was hanged for his terrible crime, none of them would be safe. She remembered him as a young boy, her childhood friend. Could he really have done something so terrible? Was she mistaken? Then she recalled his expression again as he had left her bedroom, the furious eyes and twisted mouth. There was something dark inside Clarence that had been hiding all these years.

She couldn't have Henry; he had made it clear that he didn't want her. But she needed to protect him because, trapped in his hospital bed and unable to move, he would be a helpless target.

Ava stood up straight and strode down the street. She would find Clarence and make sure he paid the price for the murder of Amelia and the crippling of Henry.

11

Ava looked at Walter and the girls while they waited for Felix Scott-Leigh to explain why he had summoned all the staff of The Orchid to his lawyer's office. It was unlikely he was planning to give them their jobs back. She loosened the scarf from around her neck, beads of sweat soaking into the material from her palms. Did the fire have to be so huge in such a small room? The lawyer sat behind his desk, fingers steepled together and a grim expression on his lined face. His gaze caught Ava's, then he looked quietly away, a flush appearing on his cheeks.

Felix, however, stared back at her from his red upholstered chair in front of the desk. His skin was white and stretched tight, eyes dark and filled with a suppressed fury that made her shudder. Why did this man hate her so?

Was his love for money so strong that he could find not an ounce of compassion for the heartbroken group of actors in front of him? Already she had seen him eye up Katie with a sneer; it was hard to hide her swollen stomach now.

Ava glanced at the chair and swallowed, raising herself on her tiptoes to ease her aching feet. It had been a long night at Drury Lane. Daisy rubbed her eyes, swaying slightly, and took Katie's hand for support. Beside them, Walter touched their backs in support, then stood still with his shoulders straight and face set.

The lawyer looked at Felix, who smiled, and Ava clenched her fists. The delay by Mr Scott-Leigh was a deliberate ploy, intended to reduce his victims to such a state they would agree to any demands. Well, she wouldn't fall for such manipulative tricks.

The lawyer cleared his throat. 'The Orchid Theatre has been burned down whilst under your care,' he said, 'causing my client significant trouble and financial loss.'

'And the death of one of my actresses,' Ava said.

'Along with causing a serious injury to my son,' Felix said, his voice flat and lacking in emotion.

Ava drew a sharp intake of breath. She had heard nothing from Henry since leaving the hospital at his request. Was he paralysed? His face, pale and scarred, haunted her dreams, causing her to wake soaked with sweat, her throat aching with unshed tears. Despite enquires, there had been no sign of Clarence and the police had done no more than take her statement and file it with a look of irritation.

'How is Henry?' she said.

'That is none of your concern. Enough harm has been caused to my son at your hands.'

'It wasn't Ava's fault the theatre burned down!' Walter said.

'I don't know what was going on at The Orchid,' Felix said, 'but Miss

Miller was in charge, and now the building is in ruins.'

Ava swayed on her feet and reached out to rest a hand against the wall. The lawyer cleared his throat and looked at her, his expression sympathetic.

'Shall we carry on?' he said.

Felix gave a sharp nod.

'Mr Scott-Leigh has graciously agreed to pay the wages of Daisy, Katie and Walter in full and final settlement of employment.'

Ava's shoulders slumped in relief. At least they would be able to pay the rent for a few weeks.

'What about Ava's wages?' Walter said.

She looked up. It was true, her name hadn't been mentioned.

'Miss Miller's wages will not be paid due to her incompetence in running the theatre. All debts in her name will also remain with her.'

Ava looked up quickly, cold sweat across her back.

'They are not my debts,' she said.

'They were taken out in the name of the theatre. I have no means to pay them. I have little more than the clothes I stand up in.'

'That's true,' Felix said. 'Yet you believed yourself a suitable match for my son. I doubt even he would be interested in you now. And especially not once you have been removed to debtors' gaol.'

'Gaol? What do you mean, gaol?' she stammered.

'Since you can't pay, a magistrate has summoned you to Marshalsea prison.'

'They can't do that without informing her!' Walter said.

'A notice was sent to her last known address. It is not our fault that she did not receive it.'

'You sent it to a burned-down theatre?'

Ava stared at the lawyer, who reddened and looked down. Felix had destroyed her entirely now. She had lost her home, her love, and now her freedom. Incarcerated in the prison, she

262

would have no means to pay the bills — as Felix knew very well. She would never get out and with the conditions in debtors' gaol being as they were, it would likely be the end of her.

'Why have you done this?' she cried. 'Why do you hate me so?'

'I have no feelings for you at all,' Felix said. 'I simply do not care.'

'I have worked hard for you.'

'You have lost me money and respect. My family gave you enough chances. I cannot be held responsible for your incompetence. If you had made a better job of running the theatre none of this would have happened.'

Ava raised a hand to her mouth, her head whirling. The heat from the fire range burned against her back as she stepped away from Felix and his insane, furious eyes. The man actually believed what he said; he held her to account for everything. How could she argue against such conviction? He would never listen to her since his own mind would not allow him to. Henry had warned her about his father, but she had paid little heed. The son had been right, though; inside the father lay something very frightening.

'We will raise the money!' Daisy said, grabbing Ava's hand, her fingers digging in.

'You can't earn that sort of money from a few parts at Drury Lane,' Felix said, his lip twisted in contempt.

'There must be a way,' Katie said. 'How could you do this? Why would you do this?' Her voice rose to a scream and she flung her hands over her face.

Ava stared at Felix's still face and staring eyes. This man would take what he wanted, then discard her. He had no loyalty or empathy. How had Henry ever grown up to have kindness and concern for others? What a childhood Henry must have had, living with this monster.

'How much money?' Walter said.

Ava moistened her lips. 'It is too much. The debts are huge and there is no way we can raise the cash.'

'And I am not taking on your debts,' Felix said.

'They are the theatre's debts.' She looked at the lawyer, who again looked down at his desk.

'You should have made it profitable. It is due to your incompetent management that money is owed at all.'

'That is not true! The place has been run down for years and it needed investment a long time before I took over.'

'Then your father is responsible. Between the two of you, my business has been ruined and you will now have to pay for it.'

'I cannot earn money from inside prison.'

'No, but it will give me satisfaction to know you are there.'

Ava shuddered. The man wanted to think of her suffering as he went about his daily business — he wasn't just selfish, he was sadistic.

'Time to go,' Felix said. Standing, he

walked over to the door and opened it. Outside, two policemen stood, arms crossed and expressions grim.

'No, you can't do this!' Walter shouted. 'She has done nothing wrong!'

Ava rested back against the wall, sweating, nausea rising from her stomach. First Clarence, and now this. How had she been unfortunate enough to be at the mercy of two such evil men?

Her eyes opened and she stared at Felix. Was it bad luck, or were they connected somehow? No, that couldn't be true. What would Felix gain from burning down The Orchid, whilst his own son slept inside? He wanted to control Henry, that was clear, but he could have no reason for wanting him dead. It must have been her assistant manager who had burned down The Orchid. Now she was starting to get paranoid, seeing conspiracies where none existed.

Ava looked at the policemen again, who stared back at her without expression. They were used to taking unfortunates to goal and would show her no compassion.

'Please don't take her!' Daisy said, her voice breaking as she sobbed. 'I can't bear to think of it!'

'It is nothing to do with us,' one of the men said. 'Come along, miss, else we'll have to handcuff you.'

Ava's gaze dropped to his belt and the cold metal cuffs hanging. She couldn't be taken out of here bound, not in front of Felix. It meant nothing to him, but she would walk tall with her head held high.

Reaching forward, she embraced the sobbing girls. 'Take care of yourselves. It won't be for long. We'll find a way,' she said.

'Miss, no!'

She looked at Walter over their heads. 'Look after them for me. Stick together, the three of you.'

'There must be something we can do!' he said.

Ava shook her head. 'There is nothing.' Then turning, she faced Felix.

267

'You know I have done nothing wrong and that those debts belong to the theatre. You might have locked me away, but I won't stay gone forever. Don't think that I will be so easily silenced.'

'You might not be easily silenced, but from inside gaol no one will hear your voice,' he said, then looked at the policemen. 'Take her away now. Her breath is polluting the office.'

* * *

Ava huddled in the prison yard, her dress gathered around her feet to dispel the rats. A reek of sweat, vomit and urine filled her nose and she moved her scarf up to cover her face. A scent of baking bread drifted from the Master's Side of the prison and her stomach rumbled, even though the lump in her throat was so painful she doubted she could have swallowed it.

A chill wind burned her face and she blinked, vision blurring. It was hard to remember a time in the last three days when she had not cried. The tears had become her constant and only companion. At night the guards forced her from her spot in the freezing prison yard into the one tiny room of the Common Side, where she huddled against the wall, surrounding by the coughing and sobbing of the other women. Babies cried, some hushed by their mothers, others left to cry by the exhausted and starving parent.

At first she had kept herself going by thoughts of the wickedness that had been done to her by Felix and Clarence. But after the first night even these thoughts had faded and she had settled into a torpor it was impossible to raise herself from. What did it matter if she died? There was nothing left to live for. She had lost everything.

A shadow appeared in front of her and she looked up. A guard stood in front of her with two familiar figures.

'Walter! Daisy!' Ava said, wiping her cheeks.

'Oh, my love,' Walter said, squatting down in the mud beside her. 'What have they done to you?' He put his arm around her and she fell against him, resting her head against his warm shoulder as she cried.

Daisy rubbed her back. 'Miss, miss, we've got to get you out of here.' The girl looked around and shuddered. 'We've money for your food and by the end of the week should have enough to get you a room on the Master's Side.'

'You need that money; there's three of you to support outside,' Ava said.

'Ava,' Walter said, drawing back, 'if we don't get you a room on the right side of the wall, you're going to be dead by the end of the month. You mustn't worry about us; there's a collection set up at Drury Lane and everyone is helping. We all know the dangers of being penniless in Marshalsea.'

Ava's eyes filled again and she slumped forward.

'When did you last eat?' Daisy said, opening a basket she'd placed on the floor. 'I remember bringing food in here for my father.'

Ava shuddered. Daisy's father had never made it out of the prison gates alive.

'First,' the girl continued, 'wipe your hands and face. You've got to stay as clean as you can to survive.'

Heat rushed to Ava's face — after three days in the same clothes she must smell like the yard mud. Taking the damp rags handed to her, she rubbed the filth from her hands. 'How is Katie?' she said.

'Doing well, learning to cook,' Daisy said, lifting out a pot covered in a thick cloth. 'It's still warm.' She put the pot of soup on Ava's lap and handed her a spoon and piece of bread.

Ava stared at the meal, her stomach clenching. But she must eat; it would have cost her friends bribes to bring it in. Raising the spoon to her lips, she swallowed. 'What happened to Amelia?' she whispered.

'She was buried yesterday. We all

went. There was a good turnout,' Walter said.

'People have been very kind.'

'Many people loved and admired you,' he said, 'and have been left horrified by the manner in which you have been treated. We're going to find a way to get you out, I promise.'

Ava nodded. In truth there was little they could do. No collection at Drury Lane could raise enough to pay her debts and to the rest of world she was just another unfortunate, fallen on bad times. Looking around the prison yard, she shuddered. 'How are you all managing?' she said.

'We're fine. Katie and I are having our banns read next week,' Walter said.

Ava spat out a mouthful of soup. 'Banns?'

'We thought it best to get married. Then she can keep the baby and carry on working, so the four of us can stay together.'

'But marriage? Isn't that a bit extreme?'

He smiled, the creases at the corners of his eyes wrinkling. 'I'm not planning on wedding anyone else and neither is Katie, so it made sense to throw our lot in together. I did always want a family, but it just never happened.'

'Katie is quite young.'

'It's a marriage in name only.'

'It was Katie's idea,' Daisy said. 'She said it was stupid us spending two lots of rent, when a bit of paper meant we could all live together. She never wants another man anyway; says she's more interested in seeing her name in lights over Drury Lane.'

Ava remembered seeing Katie and Walter together at The Orchid, arms linked. It was quite likely there was more than just practicality to Katie's plan. 'Hopefully I'll be out in time for the wedding,' she said.

'Try and eat a bit more,' Daisy said gently.

'We're going to visit Mr Henry in the hospital,' Walter said.

Ava dropped her spoon. 'You mustn't

tell him about me. He's not in a fit state to be pitted against his father.'

'He'd want to know,' Walter said firmly.

'I won't have him told. Promise me you won't tell him.'

'He's the only person we know who could lend us enough money to get you out,' Daisy said. 'We're just going to ask for a loan.'

'It's his father who put me in here, can't you understand? If Henry pays for my release he could be put in danger, and at present he is paralysed in a hospital bed. What if his father chooses to refuse to pay for his treatment? Henry could die.'

'And so could you.' Daisy looked around the stinking prison yard. 'This place is no game, Ava. I lived here for several years and my father died here. If you don't starve to death, disease or the guards will get you. There is no hope in this terrible place. You have to get out, no matter what the risk.'

'But I can't risk someone else.'

'It's time to think of yourself,' Walter said. 'Daisy is right.'

'I will think of a way,' Ava said.

'You won't, because you've given up. I saw it in your eyes when I walked across the prison yard. They have destroyed you. You mustn't let them win. Where is that famous Miller fighting spirit I used to see?'

'I have no energy and no interest,' she said, lowering her head. 'I have no means by which to fight. You and the girls are all I have in the world, my only family.'

'And are we not enough to live for?'

Tears filled Ava's eyes and she kept her head down. Her friends were not enough, because she was a burden to them now. Never before had she needed their help; always it had been she who had cared for them. It was impossible to get used to her new vulnerability.

Daisy took her hand a squeezed it. 'We need you, miss. Please don't give up. I can't bear to see you like this.'

'You must have hope, Ava darling,'

Walter said. 'Things will get better.'

'I have lost everything.'

'And you can rebuild. There was always a risk you would lose The Orchid; you must have made plans for what you wanted to do? The world does not end because one theatre has burned down. Drury Lane would employ you in an instant.'

'I don't wish to spend my life treading the boards. It is a precarious existence.'

'It is a life that Daisy and I will always have,' he said gently.

She raised her head. 'I am sorry, but it is not my future I am afraid of. I am exhausted by death and misery and fear.'

'Why are you afraid?'

Ava moistened her lips. She couldn't speak of her terror of Clarence and Felix, of her fear of never seeing Henry again. How could she tell them about the pain in her heart that caused her tears to well and her throat to numb? Was this what heartbreak felt like? This deep, dark cloud that descended the moment she opened her eyes, wrapping her mind in its thick black folds, until in desperation she willed herself to sleep once again, desperate for release.

Henry had chosen another life and she couldn't even harden her heart by thinking poorly of him, because it was understandable that he would do so. He was trapped in a hospital bed, damaged by his desire to help The Orchid and her. The memories of the last few weeks went around her mind like a carousel, but instead of horses and music, she saw his face and heard his voice.

If she knew he was well, it would help. But Henry was dangerously ill and could still die. The thought of him dying without her arms around him, of him not knowing the extent of her love for him, filled her with horror. Was he in pain? Did he suffer? Ava couldn't add to that pain by asking for help and he must never know of what his own father had done to her. She knew him too well. He was a man of courage and principle; he would stand up against his family and the results would be disastrous for him in his current weak state.

Daisy tightened her arms around her. 'Please, Ava, don't give up,' she said.

Ava looked into her friends' familiar, much-loved faces. 'Maybe,' she said, 'maybe Mr Scott-Leigh will show mercy?'

'We need a lawyer,' Walter said. 'We'll try and raise the money. You cannot be responsible for all the debts; the theatre was not yours.'

'They were taken in my name.' Ava rested back against the wall, the cold stone biting through her thin dress. She had been so blinkered and foolish, believing the only means to protect those she loved was to keep them all safe in The Orchid. Instead the theatre had been her downfall. She should never have tried to run it. Clearly she lacked the knowledge, and the world of business was a difficult one for a woman to move in.

Yet those weeks of working with Henry had been the happiest of her life. She had fit with him in a manner she never had with anyone else. If the fire hadn't happened, they would have made a success of the theatre because their different strengths complemented each other perfectly. What would happen to Henry now? Paralysed and unable to read, his life would be a bleak one. If only he could have allowed her to care for him, then they could at least have had each other.

A bell rang in the prison yard. 'We must go,' Daisy said. She took a wrapped pot from her basket and placed it on Ava's lap. 'Breakfast.'

'We'll be back tomorrow,' Walter said. 'Take care, make sure you eat, and keep hope. There are lots of people who love you, and who are willing you on.'

Ava nodded, her dry mouth forming a thanks that she wasn't sure they heard. They were right — she couldn't give up, however easy it would be to do so in this terrible place. She looked at them. 'Be careful of Clarence. I believe he is not what he seems.'

Walter nodded. 'I have suspected the same for quite some time. I have seen the houses he has been frequenting in the evenings, and they are not places good men go to.'

'Warn Henry. Say nothing of me, but tell him to be careful. I believe Clarence will try to harm him.'

'We will.' Walter squeezed her hand and rose. 'See you tomorrow, when hopefully I will bear better news.'

Ava watched them both striding through the courtyard to the prison gates.

★   ★   ★

Henry stared at the bed covers. Had the sheet moved when he wiggled his foot? Narrowing his eyes, he watched again as he tensed his limb. The bedcovers rippled and he grinned, dropping back against the pillows.

The doctor had told him that some

sensation seemed to be returning, but Henry hadn't dared hope it was true. Would he be able to walk again? He tried to shift in the bed, but his back was numb against the mattress and painful with reddened patches of bed sores. The nurse had told him his heels were also ulcerated, so they would soon try to get him moving.

Glancing to the side, he looked at the wheeled chair left beside the bed. Would that be his future? The chair's arrival had upset him; it was like a condemned man seeing his gallows. The nurse had appeared to understand, merely parking the chair beside him then quietly heading off so he could get used to the sight alone.

Henry tried to move his foot again. Please let it shift! He couldn't bear the alternative. Sighing, he closed his eyes, thoughts of Ava filling his mind as they always did when he rested. What was she doing? Treading the boards at Drury Lane, bowing to applause? One day he would go and watch her, staying hidden from view. Not yet, though; it would be too painful. The only way to stay away from her and avoid destroying her life was to avoid contact.

How had it all gone so wrong? The Orchid could have made money, since the new play was a success. But a stray cigarette or poorly banked fire had ruined all their plans. He had intended to ask Ava to marry him and to stay with her to run the theatre, the gossips be damned! But he couldn't do that now.

Footsteps echoed down the aisle and Henry turned his head. Was it time for him to try the dreaded chair? No, it wasn't a nurse; it was two people he was both desperate and fearful to see — Walter and Daisy, with their arms linked and faces pale. It would be impossible not to ask them how Ava was.

'Hello,' Daisy said. 'Do you mind us visiting?' She and Walter must be working hard, as they both looked red-eyed.

'Not at all. I would offer a seat, but the only one seems to have wheels,' Henry said. He cursed himself when the girl's eyes filled with tears. 'I'm sorry; it was meant to be light-hearted. Sit on the bed beside me; no one will see.' He patted the cover.

'How are you?' Walter said.

Henry looked at him, drawing back slightly as Walter stared into his eyes as if he were trying to tell him something.

'I am doing well. Moved my feet this morning.' He moistened his lips. 'How is Ava?'

Walter looked at Daisy.

'Is she well?' Henry asked, frowning. Why did they both look so serious?

'Fine, enjoying her new role,' Walter said, his voice stiff. 'Ava asked me to come and see you to warn you about Clarence.'

Henry looked up quickly. The mention of Clarence brought back memories of the assistant manager's furious stare. It was clear that the man was obsessed with Ava, and hated him, but surely he wasn't dangerous? He narrowed his eyes. 'Why the warning?' he said.

'Ava is suspicious of him. She thinks he had something to do with the fire,' Walter said.

'Clarence vanished that night,' Daisy said. 'And there was no body found in the building. If he cared about us, surely he would have come back to find out how we were?'

'I have wondered about him for a while,' Henry said. 'There was something disturbing about him, a lack of emotion and a dead look to the eyes. When he was warm and friendly, it always came across as an act.'

'I've not liked him for years,' Daisy said. 'But Ava was always very fond of him, so I thought it was my imagination.'

Henry shook his head. Despite her shy exterior, Daisy was a street urchin, born into London's poor and raised in a debtors' prison. He'd trust her instincts, as they were honed by the need to survive. Ava had been brought up with Clarence, and her innate kindness could prevent her seeing the bad in people. Something must have happened to change her mind, since she wasn't a woman to make unfounded accusations.

'I'll be careful,' Henry said. 'But there is no need to worry about me. What harm could come to me here? I am on a busy ward.'

Walter nodded. 'I don't think he would dare come here.'

'The more important question is whether yourselves and Ava are safe?'

'The girls and I are fine. I am lodging a few doors down from them, but in three weeks' time will be moving in to protect them. Katie and I are to marry.'

Henry stiffened his shoulders. 'Marry?'

Walter grinned. 'Don't call me out, sir. I wasn't responsible for her condition, but the marriage works for both of us and means we can stay together. We have always been a family in everything but blood.'

'You are closer than many families I know,' Henry said, and smiled. 'Including my own. I find it a comfort that Ava has you to support her and that she is doing well. Take care of her for me.'

Daisy looked at Walter and opened her mouth.

'We must leave now,' the older man said, taking her hand quickly. 'Is there anything you need?'

'Only new legs.' Henry indicated his limbs. 'Come back again, if you can. I have fond memories of my time at The Orchid and you have all become very dear to me.'

'Of course we will, sir.' Daisy squeezed his hand, then quickly turned and headed back down the ward, Walter walking afterwards.

Henry watched them go. Was Ava really all right? They had been acting strangely, as if they wanted to tell him something. Ava was a proud woman and she would never come to him in the event of crisis. Dropping his head back, he closed his eyes. How much he missed her! It was ironic that he had spent such a long time searching for a woman to fit his ideals of morality and yet had found one in the suspect world of the theatre. Ava was the most loyal and honest woman he had met, not due to her background but due to herself. Her personality wouldn't allow her to lie. Now he had lost her, and the pain of it hurt more than his injuries.

Footsteps echoed beside his bed and he quickly opened his eyes. Was it Clarence? No, it was Sidney, who smiled from the side of his bed and held out a small basket of fruit. 'Here you are,' he said, putting it on the small table. 'How are you? It took me a while to track you down.'

Henry moistened his lips. 'I'm sorry about the play. You must be very disappointed.'

'I hadn't given the play any thought. I'm sorry about Amelia. Is everyone else all right?'

'I think so. Walter and the girls are

working at Drury Lane. Ava too, I believe.'

'She isn't at Drury Lane; I've just come from there. That was how I found out where you were.'

Henry frowned, remembering the strained expression on Walter's face. 'Have you heard from her at all?' he said.

Sidney shook his head. 'I asked around, as I wanted to talk to her. To say how sorry I was.'

'Ava wouldn't leave the theatre world; it's all she knows. Maybe she's at one of the other play houses?'

'Does she not visit?'

Henry shook his head. 'It got difficult between us.'

'I noticed you kept watching her when you visited. I thought she was a lovely woman. Can you not try to sort things out?'

Henry pointed to his legs. 'I might be paralysed. Even if I am not, I won't be able to walk far. What life is that for her? No, I have to return to my family, where I can annoy them by being a burden.'

Sidney's mouth dropped open. 'You'll rot in an early grave with your family. Seriously, Henry, you musn't do that! Stay in London. You won't be a burden — you have arms; you can learn to use crutches or operate a bath-chair, with a lad pushing from behind. I know of many polio victims who manage in such a manner, with happy lives. You have the city here, with shops and entertainments.'

'I am not a rich man, not without my family to pay for me. I will be a penniless invalid, and the world for a pauper is very different to a man of means. I have only my army pension, which will not go far.'

'Henry, you are giving up! What happened to the determined solider I used to know? Run off home if you want, but at least attempt living here. Once you get back in that mansion of your father's he won't easily let you out again.'

'True.' Henry looked at his friend.

'But here I will also have to see Ava, and that will be painful.'

'Only if you let it become so. If you want to be together, then you'll find a way.'

'It's not that simple.'

'Actually, it is. You are both free to love. It is only your own fears stopping you. Ava wouldn't care about your legs, I know she wouldn't.'

'But I care enough about her not to inflict such a life on her.'

'Then you are making assumptions for her, aren't you? A man who loves and cares for her, even if he is in a bath chair, is better than an abusive husband, or loneliness. Of course you can make it work, if you want to. Don't make her decision for her.'

Henry looked down. He hadn't thought about it that way before. Ava hadn't been given a chance to decide what she wanted; rather than ordering her away, he should have talked to her.

'Could you find out where she is for me?' he said. 'Walter will know.'

'Of course.' Sidney rose from the bed and fussed with his jacket. 'By the way, there is a small theatre in the West End that is up for rent and looks a perfect place to put on my piece. It just needs a manager.'

Henry smiled. 'Thanks for the thought, but I don't think I'm in that position anymore. Not to mention that I cannot put on a play; it's not really my area of expertise.'

'It is Ava's, though.' Sidney grinned, gave a cheerful wave, and strode back down the ward.

Henry watched him go, then looked down at his legs, suddenly certain that he could feel the pressure of the blankets a little more than he had earlier. A small theatre to rent — could they do it?

★　★　★

Ava stretched out on the thin pallet mattress, her arm brushing the side of the stone wall. An icy chill from the brickwork pressed against her hand and she drew it quickly back. At least, due to the kindness of her friends at Drury Lane, she had a room. Away from the wretched despair of the Common Side communal cells, her spirits had risen a little and she gazed through the open door into the courtyard without wishing it was still night-time.

A pot of cold soup stood by her bed and she moved carefully to avoid knocking it over. A thin film of ice graced the surface, but it was all she had to eat until Daisy or Katie visited later that afternoon. All these years she had been the one caring for them, and now her very life depended on their kindness. They had told her that Henry looked better, but how much of that was an attempt at comfort she didn't know. At least they had warned him, and hopefully Henry would take it seriously.

What did the future hold for her, though? She had no means to pay back the debts and couldn't even pay for a lawyer to argue that they didn't belong to her. It had been so foolish to take them out in her own name, but at the time it had seemed like the right thing to do. True, she hadn't realised then that Felix Scott-Leigh could be such a vengeful man. How had such a monster raised such a wonderful son?

Standing in the doorway, she looked out across the prison yard. A pale sunrise streaked across the sky and vapours spread into the air from the melting frost on the prison walls. Huddled by the doors was a small family dressed in rags. The mother, a thin woman with loose brown hair, held two children silently on her lap, her face blank and exhausted. All hope had gone for them many months ago.

Picking up the soup pot, Ava stepped over the yard, the frozen mud crunching under her footsteps. Silently — you never knew what other inmates were here for — she put the soup beside them and backed away.

The morning air raised goosebumps

on her arms and she rubbed them. It would be best to return to bed until it warmed up; there was no point risking a chill. Ava stepped across the narrow walkway back into the cells. Her door was ajar and she pushed it open sharply. Had someone been in to steal her blanket whilst she had been gone? Stepping in, she checked her bed before the sound of the door slamming beside her made her jump and a hand slapped across her mouth and throat.

In shock, she froze; then, as the hand tightened around her neck, she struggled. Attempting to open her jaws, she tried to bite the foul-smelling palm that covered her mouth, but managed only a moan before it pressed harder, bringing the taste of metallic blood into her mouth. The grip over her throat strengthened and she groaned, flinging her head back repeatedly until her vision blurred. She didn't have much longer.

Jerking her leg back, she kicked hard with her prison clogs and there was a muffled cry. Ava pulled herself forward enough to turn her head and stare into the manic eyes of her ex-assistant manager. 'Clarence?' she whispered, her throat burning.

He grabbed her again and she flung herself towards the door, but he reached it first and slammed it shut. Then he pulled a long knife from his belt and smiled at her. Throwing her head back, Ava screamed loudly.

'That won't achieve anything,' Clarence said. 'There are too many people yelling in here.'

'They'll find you. Hang you.'

'Who will? You won't get found for several hours and by then I'll be back in my own cell.'

'You're a prisoner?'

'Drunk and disorderly.' He smiled.

Ava stepped back, staring at the door. Could she reach it? 'Did Felix send you?' She needed to keep him talking.

'You noticed the connection then? I thought you might. You always were bright. He doesn't know I'm here.'

'But he was responsible for the fire?'

'Oh, that place wasn't making any money! It never would. Best thing to do was claim the insurance.'

'It was your home.'

'Not for much longer!' His mouth tightened. 'I saw the way it was going with Henry Scott-Leigh. You were going to forget us all and run off with him.'

'I wouldn't have deserted you.'

'But you weren't going to marry me either, not like you promised.'

Ava swallowed. 'We were never engaged, Clarence. That was just a pretence, you know that.'

His face went still, then he flung himself forward and grabbed her jaw. 'That was not a pretence! It was your way of asking me to marry you, as you couldn't ask directly because it wouldn't have been seemly. I know you have wanted me for years. I've seen you staring.'

'I haven't stared at anyone!'

His hand clenched her face, fingernails pushing into her skin. Ava drew a

296

sharp breath and stood very still. The knife pricked her cheek.

'This isn't the way to get me to marry you.' She gave a small laugh. 'Why don't you let me go and ask properly? A girl likes a nice proposal.'

He flung her back against the wall. 'I'm not marrying you now. You're a dirty trollop, running around after other men. I need a pure wife, one who thinks only about me. Not some penniless guttersnipe.'

Ava raised a hand to her jaw, then looked down at the dots of blood on her fingers. 'Did Felix pay you to set fire to The Orchid?' she said.

'Promised to, then refused after that damned girl died. Said I'd done it wrong.'

'You were supposed to wake people up? Perform a rescue?'

Clarence stared at her, eyes sulky.

'You wanted us all to die?' Ava said, moistening her lips.

'You were all horrible to me.'

'That simply isn't true! I thought I

was your friend!'

'That's what I thought about you.' His lip protruded. 'But you betrayed me for another man.'

'I never belonged to you.'

He gave a sharp nod and looked down at his knife again. Ava followed his gaze; she had to act quickly. There was no way she could persuade him to let her go, since the man had lost his mind completely. Throwing herself forward, she grabbed the door handle and twisted it. Then an arm lashed around her neck, dragging her back. Ava wheezed for breath, eyes wide as she choked. A sharp point pressed hard against her shoulder blades. She twisted, clawing at the arm with her nails.

The door dropped open and a woman screamed. With spots in front of her eyes, Ava struggled. Had it been her who'd shouted?

Her head dropped forward and her knees buckled, then the grip loosened from her neck and she dropped to the floor. Lying still, she parted her eyelids enough to see the woman from the courtyard, holding the empty soup pot, before she closed them again.

★ ★ ★

Ava opened her eyes, then closed them again as a painful bright light burned her irises. Her neck throbbed and a sharp pain seared down her cheek. Someone spoke and she frowned; the voice was familiar. Then a warm hand squeezed hers.

'Ava, you're in hospital,' Henry said. 'It's all right now, you're safe.'

She opened her eyes slightly, desperate to see his face. Henry sat beside the bed, his legs thrust out awkwardly in front of him.

'My darling,' he said. 'I've been so worried.'

She tried to speak, but her neck hurt so badly, it was hard to form the words.

'Shhh,' he said. 'Just lie still. You've been though a terrible time.'

'Clarence?' she whispered.

'Arrested and charged. He admitted setting fire to The Orchid, and also tried to blame my father.'

Ava jerked her head off the pillow and Henry's grip on her hand tightened. 'I don't know if there will be enough evidence to charge my father, but I also believe he was connected to this. Once Walter told me that he had sent you to debtors' gaol, I knew there was nothing he would stop at. Money is his obsession. He would rather you died in gaol than have to pay the debts for The Orchid.'

'Clarence . . . ' She coughed. 'Clarence was supposed to wake us up. Your father didn't intend to kill you.'

'It was a risk he was prepared to take though. I suspect he thought it would look less like an insurance job if his own son was in the building at the time. Or maybe I was proving a burden with my various ailments. Either way, I would have been little mourned had things gone differently.'

'You mustn't go back home.'

'Of course not! I could hardly return there knowing what he's done. Stair carpets might mysteriously come loose, hunting accidents occur.' He reached forward and touched her cheek gently. 'But I had already decided to stay in London, because I couldn't bear to be parted from you. It is wrong, I know; I am a burden. But I had to let you know how I felt. It wasn't a decision I had a right to make for you.'

'I do not care what injuries you have; I don't care if you are paralysed. I have never felt so loved and happy with anyone before. Being with you is like coming home after all these years. Even The Orchid never gave me the sense of belonging that you do. I couldn't bear to be without you.'

'I didn't want to inflict myself on you, although it almost destroyed me to walk away.'

'You couldn't inflict yourself on me.' Ava swallowed, and raised a hand to her throat.

'Forgive me, you are in no condition for a conversation such as this!' He grabbed a glass of water from the night table and held it to her lips. She gulped, the cool liquid soothing her painful throat. Was it true that Henry was going to be with her?

'I have some feeling back in my legs,' he said. 'It is likely that I won't be paralysed, although I will always have a degree of damage.'

'I am sorry.' She squeezed his hand. 'It makes no difference to the way I feel about you. As long as you are with me, I do not care.'

'How would you like to run a theatre?'

'Pardon?'

'Sidney has spotted one up for hire and I have sufficient funds to pay the first few months' rent. We have a play and a willing cast. Will you join us?'

'A theatre? Put on the play again?' Her mouth fell open. 'But what about my debts? I am still a prisoner.'

'You aren't. I had sufficient words

302

with my father to convince him that paying off your debts on your behalf would be the safest option for him. He suspects I know of his underhand dealings.'

'So I am free?'

'You are, although I am horrified at what you must have suffered in that place. Why on earth didn't you tell me what had happened?'

'I was worried he would refuse to pay for your medical treatment.'

'At least you are safe now and Clarence is awaiting trial as he deserves. I never warmed to him; there was something dark inside his mind.'

Ava nodded, her eyes filling with tears as she remembered the boy she had known. The child she would mourn, but not the twisted man he had become. 'What will happen to him?'

'He was caught trying to strangle you, so he will be hanged.' She shuddered. 'I'm sorry, Ava, but while that man lives you will never be safe. He is obsessed with controlling you. Let him go and we will start a new life in our theatre, along with Walter and the girls.'

He leaned down and pressed his lips to hers, kissing her gently, then harder as she responded. Reaching up, Ava slid her arms around his neck, breathing in his scent and feeling his warmth against her body. She didn't know what would happen in the future — whether Henry would walk again, if they could make a success of a theatre — but she did know that without this man beside her, she would be nothing. They enhanced each other, she was a better person with him, and she couldn't imagine her life without him in it.

Epilogue

'Ready, girls?' Ava said, looking at the clock. 'Curtain up in ten minutes.'

Daisy grinned from under her ringlets. 'All set, Mrs Scott-Leigh.'

Ava laughed. 'I think it will take a while to get used to that one! I still think of myself as a 'miss'.'

'It was such a wonderful day.' Katie danced across the room, then stopped at the sound of a cry. 'Have I time to feed her before I'm on stage?'

'If you're quick.' Ava crossed to the cradle in the corner of the dressing room and lifted out a swaddled baby.

A knock echoed from the door. 'All right to come in?' Walter said.

'We're all dressed, it's only your wife who isn't,' Ava said.

'I doubt she'd mind!' Walter strode in, dressed in a dapper Regency costume. 'Full house out there tonight.

We're doing well.'

Ava smiled as he stopped by Katie and dropped a kiss on top of her head. The marriage of convenience had turned into a true love match. She turned at the sound of footsteps from the auditorium at the end of the corridor; their audience had arrived. In this smaller, modern theatre, the comedies and dramas she selected had proved so successful, seats were booked up weeks in advance. She'd employed a second assistant manager to help her, along with several new permanent cast members.

Briefly she remembered Clarence, and her lips pressed tightly together. He had received the fate that Henry had predicted, cursing her until the moment they put the rope around his neck. There had been something rotten inside her childhood friend and it hadn't been her fault — he always would have turned out the way he had.

The door opened again and Henry walked in, pausing to rest on his two canes. 'All set?' He smiled.

'I'd better get on stage.' Taking a deep breath, Daisy squared her shoulders and walked out the door. Ava followed, pausing beside her husband to squeeze his hand, as a roar of excitement came from the audience. With a job and a man she loved, truly she was blessed!

THE END

We do hope that you have enjoyed reading this large print book.

Did you know that all of our titles are available for purchase?

We publish a wide range of high quality large print books including:
Romances, Mysteries, Classics
General Fiction
Non Fiction and Westerns

Special interest titles available in large print are:
The Little Oxford Dictionary
Music Book, Song Book
Hymn Book, Service Book

Also available from us courtesy of Oxford University Press:
Young Readers' Dictionary
(large print edition)
Young Readers' Thesaurus
(large print edition)

For further information or a free brochure, please contact us at:
Ulverscroft Large Print Books Ltd.,
The Green, Bradgate Road, Anstey,
Leicester, LE7 7FU, England.
Tel: (00 44) 0116 236 4325
Fax: (00 44) 0116 234 0205

SUZI LEARNS TO LOVE AGAIN

Patricia Keyson

Upon meeting troublesome pupil Tom's father, Cameron, young schoolteacher Suzi feels an immediate attraction. She is determined not to be drawn into a relationship, knowing she would feel unfaithful to her late husband; but the more time Cameron and Suzi spend together, the more they are captivated by each other. Suzi rediscovers deep emotions, though she agrees with Cameron that Tom must come first . . . But how long can Suzi hide her love for Cameron?

THE DUKE & THE VICAR'S DAUGHTER

Fenella J. Miller

The Duke of Edbury decides he must marry an heiress if he is to save his estates. So far he has managed to stay out of the clutches of the predatory mothers who spend the Season searching for suitable husbands for their daughters. The god-daughter of his aunt, Lady Patience, might be a suitable candidate, and he is persuaded to act as a temporary guardian to both her and her cousin, Charity Lawson. When Charity and Patience exchange places, the fun begins . . .

A PLACE OF PEACE

Sally Quilford

When Nell participates in a transatlantic house-swap, going to stay in New England on the beautiful Barratt Island for three months, she hopes to escape the shame she left behind in Derbyshire. She soon meets gorgeous police chief Colm Barratt — and scheming socialite Julia Silkwood, whose husband's health seems to be failing suspiciously quickly. With Nell's overactive imagination running riot, and her past about to catch up with her, she fears she could lose Colm forever.

LOST AND FOUND

Wendy Kremer

Ex-nautical engineer turned treasure hunter Alex Harding is about to embark on a salvage operation in the Caribbean, hunting for booty from a sunken ship. Auctioneer Zoe hopes to gain exclusive auction rights to his finds for her company. They're immediately attracted to each other, but Alex seems to be involved with Maria, and Zoe doesn't want to end up with a womanizer. There's more than buried bullion at stake — love is also up for the asking. But who will win the final bid?

A TENDER CONFLICT

Susan Udy

Believing a local meadow to be the site of an ancient battle, Kristin Lacey and her small band of eco-protesters set up camp there in order to fend off ruthless property developer Daniel Hunter and his plans for 'executive' homes. Then Kristin discovers her mother has a secret that could put a spanner in the works — and, to make matters worse, she finds herself increasingly attracted to the very man who should be her enemy. When her feelings betray her, is she playing straight into his hands?